Applejack & Bat Masterson

TRINIDAD'S LAW

CHARLIE STEEL
Tale-Weaver Extraordinaire

Applejack & Bat Masterson

TRINIDAD'S LAW

CHARLIE STEEL
Tale-Weaver Extraordinaire

Condor Publishing, Inc.
Lincoln, Michigan

Applejack & Bat Masterson: TRINIDAD'S LAW
by Charlie Steel

December 2017

Library of Congress Control Number: 2017964106

ISBN-13: 978-1-931079-32-7

Condor Publishing, Inc.
PO Box 39
123 S. Barlow Road
Lincoln, MI 48742
www.condorpublishinginc.com

Printed in the United States of America

Bartholemew William Barclay "Bat" Masterson
(November 26, 1853 – October 25, 1921)
the MAN!

This book is dedicated to Bat Masterson who, along with his brothers, went WEST and made a name for himself as a frontiersman, a gambler, a shootist, and a lawman. He was friend and peer to the famous men of his time, especially Wyatt Earp, Doc Holliday, and Teddy Roosevelt. Then, when it suited him, Masterson went east to pursue his desire to be a sports reporter and boxing promoter, using his fame and contacts to secure an appointment as U.S. Marshal from President Teddy Roosevelt.

HISTORICAL NOTE

For the advancement of this story, the author has taken certain liberties with the history of Trinidad, Colorado regarding Reverend Pedro Juan Munnecom, real name Peter Munnecom, a priest from Holland. He actually arrived in Trinidad on June 24, 1866, and was appointed by Reverend John Baptist Lamy, Bishop of Santa Fe. Father Munnecom remained as priest until November 19, 1875. He then retired and stayed in the area for a while, before returning to Holland.

The church was not so well organized in those early years. Land grant holder Don Felipe Baca, thought to be the wealthiest man in New Mexico and Trinidad, Colorado, was responsible for advertising land and encouraging members of the Catholic community to move to the town. The first Catholic church there was named Santisma Trinidad (Holy Trinity) and that is what gave the town of Trinidad its name. It is recorded that it was built of earthen walls and contained dirt floors. Again the author embellishes as he envisions Santisma Trinidad as being an exquisite and awe inspiring earthen structure such as he has visited in his many travels---most especially the Acoma tribe's San Estevan Del Rey Mission Church on the Sky City Mesa, in New Mexico.

Historical records claim that in the year 1883, during Bat Masterson's election as town marshal, Jesuit priests administered the gospel to 27 different villages in the area, traveling a hundred mile circuit by horseback, taking a vow of poverty and living in primitive conditions. The Sisters of Charity coming from Ohio to Trinidad as early as 1869 continued to offer a public school for the community.

When the author first learned of the priest Peter Munnecom, and the fact that this missionary was appointed by a Bishop from Santa Fe to the annoyance of it parishioners, it gave an incredible opportunity to write about a real priest with interesting character flaws. In those nine years Munnecom was a priest, he was known to gamble and accomplish business deals for his own benefit. It was also unique to learn that this priest from Holland, to the chagrin of a mostly Spanish speaking congregation, did not speak Spanish. What could be more perfect than to write about a real priest in Trinidad who, against devout tradition of the time, had worldly ways? This is a historical Western, but in this case, the writer has adjusted the calendar to further entertain the reader.

Therefore, this particular historical explanation and disclaimer about the story is presented. The author's deviation from the timeline in no way is intended to diminish the work and dedication of the Sisters of Charity or of the Holy Fathers. Understanding that, the author wishes you an enjoyable journey into Applejack Martin and Marshal Bat Masterson's West.

Chapter 1

*In this life, struggle and hard work **only sometimes**
equates to happiness, but usually, that is all we have.
(Charlie Steel)*

Jack Martin got his name, Applejack, when he was seven
years old. He found his way into his father's hard cider
and drank it down. His mother said that was the happiest
day of his life.

Standing at the edge of the cliff, Applejack began to
climb. It was a small mountain plateau strewn with
granite boulders—a pile of rocks thrust up from some
volcanic upheaval that occurred millions of years before.
The mountain was formed long ago when dinosaurs
roamed the earth and the beginnings of man were nothing
but little furry creatures running under the feet of great
raptors.

Applejack was only vaguely aware that such animals
once existed or that the rocks under his feet were so
ancient. After a brisk fifteen minutes and heavy
breathing, the young man came to the flat top. He walked
to the steep edge, found a seat, and looked down. All
through his young life, at times of conflict, this was
something he was prone to do. And now was the greatest
conflict of all; for his mother lay down there in her grave,
finally come to rest next to his father, both dead after a

prolonged life of struggle and hard work. And still the small ranch was nothing but a shallow spring, sparse grass, enumerable piles of rocks, and a few sickly cattle. Applejack made up his mind that although it had fed his parents, the homestead was not worth keeping. He would sell the cattle, ride away, and leave the wooden crosses to wither in the wind, as the ranch house had done all these many years.

Applejack sat quietly and gazed out over the wide-open spaces. A hot western breeze blew across his face, and he removed his sombrero, wiped his wet brow with a sleeve, and ran a hand over his head to brush back light brown hair. He stared at the distant horizons. He had always wondered what magic they held, and now, finally, he would find out for himself.

It was not difficult to saddle the buckskin stallion he had captured and tamed not so many years back. Running the old bull, four cows, calves, and three steers to the little corral in Badito wasn't hard either. Bucky was quick to chase a tail, and the cattle minded all the way in. Selling the beef at a fair price was another matter. There was the grocery store that took the three steers at eight dollars a head. The full-grown beef were sold as cheap as it got. The calves would be butchered that day, and they went for a lousy three dollars. Thirty-six dollars wasn't much more than a month's wages.

The four cows, with new halters and lead ropes, their udders full of milk, went to various families for ten dollars a head. *And good luck trying to milk those critters,* thought Jack.

Applejack counted out the money he had left, seventy dollars. The bull sat in the pen, and no one would take it.

Finally, a wandering Ute, as gaunt as a hitching rail, took the brute off the young rancher's hands for a half-smile and firm handshake. Applejack watched as the old Indian herded the big bull out of the pen on foot, using a stout stick. The former warrior directed the bull's forward passage by a clout on its rear end. It was going to be a long walk back to the Ute's camp as the skinny, big-horned brute was taking to darting left or right, but seldom straight ahead.

Money in the pocket of his faded canvas pants, Applejack headed for the General Store and spent an hour making careful purchases. He brought the merchandise to the counter and packed them in a new pannier. His mother's bay mare, still in the corral at the ranch, would carry the supplies.

"Mr. Baker," Applejack said to the store owner. "I'll be back shortly with my packhorse to pick up this here order."

"You leaving us, Jack?" asked Baker.

"I reckon its time I move on and see what the rest of the world's like."

"Sorry about your Ma, lad. But take my word, that spread of yours may not be the best patch of ground, but it's yours. It would be a shame to up and leave all that hard work your Ma and Pa put into the place."

"That's why I'm going. It wore them out before their time, and I'll be looking for something different."

"There's nothin in this world that's for free, son. And that's a fact."

"What do I owe you, Mr. Baker?"

"With the new Winchester, ammunition, and supplies, that'll be thirty-six dollars even."

3

Applejack Martin rode his buckskin slowly back towards the homestead. Both sides of the road were dotted with endless cedar trees. All of varying sizes, adding green to a sweeping landscape of yellow grass as far as the eye could see. To the south the twin Spanish Peaks rose nearly three miles in the dry air. He wanted to savor this last journey to the ranch, but it didn't take long. Behind the faded gray cabin loomed the peak of Greenhorn Mountain, and some distance to the left and much closer to the ranch house, stood Badito Cone. Entering the yard, his mother's bay whinnied a greeting. Using a rope, Jack caught the mare, applied bridle and lead, and then led her out of the corral and tied her to the hitch rail in front of the homestead.

Entering the cabin one last time, Applejack looked around. The young man knew there was no sane person in a hundred miles that would give one thin dime for the place. He laid a hand across the scarred crude wooden table his father had made so many years before. The possessions in the cabin were similarly made, and leaving them behind would be no loss. The additions to the home were the two bedrooms, his and the parent's. Both doors were open, and he could see the faded mirror on his mother's dresser, the two beds, and the pitchers and basins on the night stands. The young man noted the items he would leave behind. The three oil lamps, though worn, would be of good service as well as the furniture, should someone choose to inhabit the old homestead. The open stone fireplace would remain in his memory forever, every stone laid by his father's hands long before Jack was born.

The young Westerner had already chosen what he

would take, and that was packed away in his saddlebags or upon his person. From his mother, he kept a silver locket, a tiny framed tintype wedding picture of his parents, his mother's skillet, a fork, and a spoon. From his father, he kept his silver-plated pocket watch, a hunting knife, and a .36 Army cap and ball pistol. Taking one last look, Applejack closed the front door. Putting foot to stirrup, he rose into the saddle, the lead rope of the mare in his right hand and reins to Bucky in his left. Leaving the hardscrabble ranch was easier than he thought, and when he rode down the trail to the main track to town, he only looked back once.

Carrying the pannier from the general store and tying it on the mare's back was a simple task. The pack wasn't particularly heavy, but the mare started to hump her back and buck. She managed one kick of her rear hooves. The snap of the lead rope in the mare's face ended the protest before it started.

"I know you've been idle and lazy, old girl," said Applejack. "But that's going to change. It's a fifty-mile ride to Trinidad."

The hooves of both horses pounded on the hard adobe ground and rang against an occasional granite stone. For the first time in his twenty-year life, Applejack Martin felt exhilarated. He was riding south toward an unknown future. He may worry about how he would make his living but he would not waste another moment on that dry ranch of his parents. He knew not what he would do, but he would not worry about a failing crop, or if rain would make the grass grow, or if the spring would run dry.

Like nearly every day during the year in Southern

Colorado, the sun was up, shining down through an azure blue sky. There were the open and vast distances that only the dry western air could create. The huge dome of blue seemed endless and spread wide, horizon to horizon, with just an occasional cloud. Across the vast distance, black volcanic mountains rose up, and the two highest mountains always visible were the twin Spanish Peaks with the last caps of dirty gray snow. It was June, and the temperature was warm. Today's destination on the way to Trinidad would be Aguilar. There was a little stream there. His father had taken him to the place once, and the son still remembered.

Applejack rode Bucky through the warm day, never stopping. The bay mare of his mother's occasionally protested and tugged constantly on the lead rope. Jack's arm tired, and he tied the rope to the horn of his saddle and ignored the jerking of the mare carrying his pack of supplies. From time to time, the young man removed his sombrero and ran fingers through his wet hair, wiping sweat from his brow with his right forearm.

"We won't stop for lunch," said the cowboy, "but I guess we could all do with a drink. Whoa, Bucky, steady now."

Applejack dismounted, undid the lead rope, removed his large canteen, and retied the lead. Pulling the cork, the young man drank thirstily from the tepid water that tasted a bit like metal. Then he sloshed a fair amount into his hat, hung the canteen strap to the horn, and went forward to offer water to his buckskin.

"That's it, old friend," said the youthful adventurer, "drink it up."

The stallion sucked down the water and snorted.

"Boy, some day you and the bay are going to make me some fine foals, just as soon as I figure out where we're going to settle. I reckon I won't give up cowboying forever, just not on a place with no grass."

The young man gave water to the mare in a similar manner, put on his wet chapeau, mounted, and preceded south along the main trail. This was a wide-open country. As he rode, to his left he saw endless miles of yellow grassland dotted with jumping cholla stretched in hills and valleys to the far horizon. To his right was the beginning of jagged volcanic rock that rose high and black against the blue sky. Occasionally groups of pronghorn walked along the open range, lazily grazing on grass. Others were lying down in the heat of the day.

By nightfall, Applejack reached Aguilar, and he was tired and thirsty. Leaving the trail, he rode down a hill onto Main Street. This was a Mexican community, and most of the buildings were adobe. There was a water trough next to a large building. The rider stopped, stepped down, and, holding lead and reins, he let his horses drink. He watched them thirstily suck up the water. When he thought they had enough, he pulled them away and led both mounts down the street to a cantina. He tied the horses to the hitching post in front. Guitar strumming came to the young man's ears, and he hungrily anticipated a good meal and a drink.

Applejack stepped up onto the boardwalk and through the open heavy doorway of the cantina. The man playing guitar by himself in the corner, looked up, hesitated, and then continued on after a brief glance at the stranger. In another part of the room sat several men, their large sombreros resting on empty tables as they drank from heavy stone cups. At the bar was a blocky, bearded and tough-looking Mexican. He was speaking to an attractive dark-haired young woman. A man with a wide waist came from around the bar and up to Jack as the young man picked an empty table and sat down.

"Sí, señor?" said the server.

"Could I have something to eat and drink?" asked Jack.

"We have frijoles with tortillas."

"Do you have lemonade or sarsaparilla?"

"Sí, lemonade."

"I'll take it."

The waiter held a towel in one hand and as he leaned on the table and wiped, he whispered. "Señor, the man at the bar is a mean one, a very bad bandito, and he has been drinking. Please, eat quickly and go."

Applejack slowly turned to look toward the bar and saw the dark-haired fellow already staring at him. The man was dressed in colorful trousers tucked into high-topped boots with large Mexican spurs. Around his waist he wore a carved holster and belt, and silver grips gleamed along with a row of .45 cartridges. The man's massive chest was partially covered with an open yellow shirt and a shiny brown leather vest. He held his mouth in a grimace that exposed several gold teeth.

The server brought the food and drink on a tray. Applejack held a coin out. It was taken and change was given. Hungry, Jack used a fork and dug in, eating the beans quickly. He picked up the tortillas and chewed them down. The lemonade came in a large glass and it was cool, sweet, and refreshing. All the time he ate, Jack could feel the eyes of the big man upon him. The subdued notes from the guitar and low chatter from the men at an opposite table was uniquely pleasant.

There was the scrape of boot heels stepping across the stone floor and Applejack, finishing his meal and a long last gulp of his drink, began to rise.

"What's the hurry, Gringo," said the tough-looking Mexican. He spoke English in a heavy accent and words slurred from drink.

"I'm finished," Jack replied.

"What brings you here?"

"I'm on my way to Trinidad."

The young man was on his feet, and instinctively he knew this was trouble he could not avoid.

"Gringo, I don't like you in my cantina."

"No problem, I'll go."

"But not on your feet!"

The drunken Mexican reached out with a thick arm and hand and grabbed the young man's shirt. It ripped as Jack was thrust forward and then a big fist smashed into his mouth and chin. It lifted Applejack up and backwards to fall heavily on his side on the stone floor. Dazed, the young man lay nearly unconscious, and then he felt the kick of a boot into his belly. Doubled over, he did his best to protect himself from further kicks.

"This will teach you to come in here."

Gathering what strength was left to him, Jack rolled over and came to his feet. Swaying, holding his belly, and feeling blood drip from his chin, he looked through teary eyes at the drunken fellow before him.

"Now use that gun of yours, Gringo, or get out."

Swaying, Jack held himself in as he did his best to walk toward the door.

"Haw, haw, haw!" The laughter was loud and forced from other patrons.

"Look at the Gringo!" sneered the big Mexican.

"No seas muy duro con él, es sólo un crío," said the bartender.

"Kid or not, I'll be as hard on him as I want," yelled the bandito. "I like beating up gringos. I told you before, Luis, mind your own business."

Walking through the door, the young man held in his pain and shame. Stepping off the boardwalk, he gathered reins and the mare's lead. He put a foot in a left stirrup and pulled himself onto the saddle. Feeling for the right stirrup, and leaning heavily forward, Applejack kicked the sides of his mount and guided the two horses up the street. Behind, shouting and raucous laughter of the tough Mexican echoed toward him and between the adobe buildings.

Through fat lips and an aching jaw, Applejack complained to Bucky. "Old fellow, that didn't go well. First day out and I find what I'm made of."

Riding steadily west and along the base of the Spanish Peaks, the cowboy continued to endure the pain of the physical blows and what had happened to him. What hurt worse was the shame and humiliation. He could have drawn on the drunken man, but he was no gunslinger. All he had ever used his Pa's pistol for was to shoot varmints and an occasional rabbit.

"But hang it, Bucky. It's sure hard to live with how this worked out."

Chapter 2

Applejack rode the buckskin up the trail and pulled the increasingly reluctant bay mare along, the pain in the young man's jaw increased, and it hurt every time he moved his mouth. His teeth also hurt where he was punched, and all he wanted to do was find some kind of shelter away from any interference. Leaving the trail, Jack guided both horses south across a wide-open field. By the time he reached a cluster of trees, the moon was beginning to rise. Before the trees was the glistening of water, and surrounding the small pond was a herd of elk. As Applejack approached, the herd began moving off. They walked quickly and effortlessly, forming into a long line, each large animal holding its head high as they began to run. Despite a hundred or so, they made little noise as they disappeared.

Applejack dismounted, let the animals drink from the edge of the pond, and when they had their fill, he led them a short way into the trees. He stripped the pack from the mare and then took his saddle, rifle, bedroll, and saddlebags from the buckskin. Jack hobbled both horses, and for good measure, tied ropes to halters and the other ends to trees. Given the way he was feeling, he figured it would take several days to recover. It appeared game was plentiful, and he would have no trouble hunting meat if and when he could ever chew again.

Spreading out the bedroll next to the saddle, he placed rifle and pistol on it. Lying down, he covered himself with a blanket and tried to find sleep. The throbbing pain in his jaw and mouth would not let him, so he laid there, conscious and thinking dark thoughts. Just a few yards away, Bucky, his bit pulled from his mouth, was cropping grass and chewing. His teeth made loud chomping and grinding noises.

"Couldn't sleep with that noise anyway, Bucky," said Applejack. "How come you came all the way over here? The grass greener next to me, boy?"

Now what am I going to do, he thought. *First time out and I get punched in the face. Maybe I'm not good for anything other than herding cattle. Maybe not even that. Who would hire me anyway? Ma, Pa, if you're lookin' down, I could use a little help here.*

By the third day, the pain began to subside. Applejack shot a cottontail with his Pa's pistol and was surprised he got it first shot. He cooked it over a small fire and then quickly stomped out the blaze. A little salt and the stringy meat tasted good. As he cleaned up camp and got ready to leave, there was the sudden pounding of hooves, and a horse came trotting through the trees. It passed by the supply pack, and a man fell out of the saddle. He landed heavily onto thick grass. The animal continued a few lengths, its reins got caught in brush, and it came to a halt.

Applejack stared in surprise, and raced to the horse.

"Easy, boy, no one's going to hurt you," the young man crooned, and then tied reins to a tree.

The person lay where he fell. When Jack went to him, he discovered an older, well-dressed fellow. His bearded face was weathered and deeply tanned. There was blood high up on the left shoulder, and it looked like it had been bleeding for a long time. The shirt, vest, and even his pants were soaked. The wounded man's bandanna was missing, so taking his own, Applejack stuffed it in the gunshot hole and held it there. It only took a moment before it was sodden with blood. If this fellow was to live, the bleeding must be stopped.

Acting quickly, Applejack ripped away the man's shirt. The shoulder revealed a deep bullet hole continuously welling up blood. Holding the kerchief, Jack raised the fellow up and looked at his bare back. On the other side was a small bulge. It appeared that the bullet was just under the skin. He took up his knife and made a slice, and the bullet popped out and into his right hand, along with a gush of blood.

"Got to stop the bleeding," said Applejack.

Tearing a section from the fellow's shirt, the young man stuffed the cloth into the back wound. Lowering him down, he pushed the blood-soaked kerchief further into the shoulder wound. Going to the cold fire pit, Applejack pulled some tinder from a pile and lit it. The fire caught, rose up, and larger pieces were added until a good-sized flame was blazing. The younger man placed his hunting knife in the flames and waited until the metal turned red. Then, picking up the blade, he hurried to the wounded stranger. Wiping the blood away, Jack pressed down hard, and skin sizzled and burned. He continued pressing firmly, and the burning flesh did not smell pleasant.

"God help me," said the young man.

Lifting the blade, Applejack looked at the wound. The bleeding had stopped. Returning to the fire Jack repeated the process. Applying the red hot metal to the back wound, he held it a briefer time, and the flow of blood ceased.

"Touch and go, I'd say," said Applejack. "Feller, you lost a lot of blood and you sure look gray."

The stranger's horse nickered. Jack untied it and led it to the pond. He let the mount drink and while he did so, he looked closely at the animal.

"You've got some blood in you, hoss. I bet you're a runner. And look at that saddle! Mighty fancy."

When he thought the horse had enough, he led it back to camp. Taking the rope from his hobbled buckskin, he tied the thoroughbred off. Pulling the bit, he removed saddle, bedroll, and saddlebags. There was a fancy rifle in a scabbard, and he leaned that against a tree. Using the man's saddle for a pillow and stretching the fellow's bedroll out, Jack gently dragged him over and onto it.

"Well, Mister," said the young cowboy. "I've done all I can, except maybe trying to get you to drink a bit of water. Only time will tell."

It didn't take long for the fevered and unconscious westerner to start mumbling in his sleep. Over a twenty-four hour period, the stranger revealed where and how he got his money.

"So Snyder, you thought could take all the payroll? Here's a bullet to change your mind."

Applejack, hearing this, moved the outlaw's pistol, rifle, and saddlebags further from reach. Taking off the stranger's boots, he found a knife in one, and a derringer in the other. His belt buckle turned into some kind of knife, and around the man's waist, he found a heavy money belt. These he hid under a tree and covered with brush.

The fever seemed to increase, and it took all the

patience Jack had to wet the fellow's lips and try to get him to drink. The next night, Jack watched the waterhole and shot a small doe. This he cut up and he cooked the best pieces, salted them liberally, and packed the meat in canvass. A piece of the loin he smashed into paste and boiled in a frying pan, making a venison broth for the wounded man. He managed to get the outlaw to swallow a few spoonfuls.

The gunman lay unconscious in fevered delirium, and Applejack listened in interest. The wounded man talked about a farm and about caring for his ailing mother. He rambled on and on about her death. "Ma, I'm sorry. If I had money, you wouldn't be buried in this lousy box. I know it ain't right, but as sure as I'm breathin, I swear, you're gonna get a grand headstone and a fancy casket. You'll see; we won't never be poor again." It told Jack a lot about his fevered guest, and his strong feelings toward the fellow softened. As with his own mother and father, he knew that constant toil and poverty could indeed be hard.

On the evening of the fourth day, the man awoke.

"Who are you?" asked the outlaw.

"They call me Applejack. Relax, I took out the bullet, and it looks like you'll recover. Here's some broth. It'll help you gain strength."

Before the man could speak, Jack put a spoon to his lips, and the man swallowed a number of mouthfuls.

"I won't be forgettin," began the wounded man, struggling to raise his head.

"Hush now, save your strength."

With that, the sick man lay back, closed his eyes, and for the first time, slept calmly. Jack watched him and felt his forehead, and the fever seemed to be subsiding. In the morning the outlaw awakened, and when he did, Applejack was waiting, providing more broth. The wounded man ate and drank his fill. Asking to be propped up, the next questions out of the man's mouth were not hard to guess.

"Where's my guns?" was the first question.

"Safe."

"And my money belt?"

"Hidden."

"Where are..."

"No need to worry," said Jack, "I won't be taking your things. I just sort of wanted to be sure you wouldn't be doing me harm before I give them back."

"Why did you do it?"

"You mean..."

"You know what I mean. Save some stranger. It would have been easier to..."

"No different than taking care of some stray. I'm sure you would have..."

"No, kid...I would have taken your things and kept on ridin."

"Perhaps you don't remember, but my name's Applejack—and yours?"

"For the moment...you can call me...Bill Smith."

"All right...Bill...you just relax and recover. If you think you can, I got some solid meat to eat."

"What I want now," said Bill, "is a good hot cup of coffee. And say," said the outlaw, moving uncomfortably to a better position, "what did you do? Brand me?"

"Coffee's coming right up. Guess you could say I did. It was the only way I could stop the bleeding."

Over the next week, a sort of friendship built up between the older man and the younger one. Not used to trusting people, there were moments when harsh statements escaped the outlaw's lips and then, remembering himself, the hard fellow did his best to find better words. Now wearing a sling to hold his left arm, Bill stood up and tried walking around. Eventually, he approached Applejack.

"Boy," said Bill, "I think it's time we have a talk."

"Yes?"

"I've been around fevered men before. Tell me, what did I blurt out?"

Jack knew that holding back would only make the situation worse.

"You talked about a payroll robbery and someone named Snyder."

"I thought so. Is that why you hid my guns and money?"

"I suppose...but I had no intention of holding them back...just that I didn't..."

"Want to get hurt?"

"Yes."

"Well?"

Going to a certain tree, the young man kicked away brush and then bent down and pulled out saddlebags and a rolled piece of canvas. Bringing them back to the fire, he undid the roll and exposed pistol and holster, the money belt, boot knife, derringer, and rifle.

"Thanks boy. I appreciate it. Now tell me, what's that antique you're wearing on your hip? It looks to me to be a .36 Army Colt."

"It was my father's."

"That explains a lot." Bill bent down and, with one hand, dexterously undid a strap on one side of his saddlebag. He reached inside and pulled out a nickel-plated Colt .45, holster, and belt. Along with it he found a box of cartridges and stood up.

"You take these and put your father's keepsake away. Have a man-sized weapon."

"I don't know what to say," said Jack, picking up the pistol and gun rig.

"Don't say nothin, kid. What you did for me, no man can repay. Now tell me, do you know how to use it?"

"I shot a few varmints and rabbits with Pa's cap and ball. That's it."

"With every shot?"

"Not hardly. About one out of five."

"If you like, while I'm recovering, I can give you a few tips. But if you really want to get good, you'll have to make a trip to town and buy more shells."

"I was going to talk to you about that. We're gettin low on supplies. And to tell you the truth, I have reason for learnin how to…"

Bill laughed. "Someone did you wrong, did they?"

"Yes."

"This is the West, and if a man is willing to carry, he's a fool if he don't learn how to shoot."

"When do you want me to go for supplies?"

"I'll give you some money, and we can make a list. One thing I've been hankerin for is a good airtight of peaches. And maybe some peppermint for my sweet tooth, and…tobacco. You're the first young feller I ever met that don't smoke. Somethin's wrong with that."

"My Ma didn't favor tobacco and for that matter,

alcohol. She made me promise that I wouldn't..."

"Jack!" laughed Bill. "You're also the first feller I ever met to keep such word. We'll see what you do once you get among women and other men."

"Maybe."

"No maybe about it. From what you told me, you haven't seen or done much except work your ranch and take care of your Ma. Mind you...I ain't sayin that's a bad thing. 'Cause if she hadn't taught you what she did, I have a feelin I wouldn't be here at 'tall.'"

"I reckon."

"Haw! Applejack, I be durned if you ain't the first feller I took to in a long time. Now grab a pencil and let's start on that list. You do know how to read and cipher?"

Chapter 3

For more than a month the two men camped out in the tree line, not too far from the town of Aguilar. Applejack made sure to purchase supplies in the early morning and thus avoid any trouble with the Mexican bandit. Taking their horses far from camp, they found a rock cliff, and there the outlaw began to instruct the young man on how to shoot.

"Forget all that aiming stuff," said the man who called himself Bill. "If you have plenty of time, sure, you can draw and aim your pistol; but in the business I'm in, there's no time for that nonsense. The trick is to draw, point, and fire; all without aiming or delay. Your life will depend on how quick you can point and shoot. So let's get started."

The gunfighter, left arm in a sling, handed Applejack a silver dollar.

"Now take that nail and hammer I told you to get, and pound a hole through that dollar and fix it to that tree in front of the cliff."

"Is that what I'm going to aim at?" asked Jack.

"I told you, no aiming! Don't you listen, boy? You're gonna draw and shoot just like pointing a finger. Before I'm through with you, it's going to be second nature. You'll be able to do it in your sleep…and, more importantly…hit what you're looking at."

Day after day, Applejack did as he was told and day after day his ability to hit the silver dollar fixed to the tree seemed to get worse. Behind the tree, there were dozens of indentations where his bullets struck rock. Discouraged, there were many times when Applejack wanted to quit, but Bill wouldn't let him.

"Here," said Bill. "This is how you do it!"

With his right hand, Bill pulled his pistol and fired. The clink of lead against metal was distinctly heard as the bullet hit the silver dollar with the first shot.

"Once I get this arm out of a sling, I'll show you how to fan. For you to do it, I'll have to do some filing on your Colt. For now, you just keep practicing. I've got plenty of money for ammunition. The key is to get used to the weight and the feel of the thing. Get your muscles and eyes to work together."

Not sure he would ever get it right, Applejack practiced and practiced. Back at camp, late into the evening, Bill had the young man continue drawing without firing. The outlaw made him do this over and over. By the fifth week, Jack was beginning to hit part of the tree, but only once did he hit the coin. Then Bill removed the sling and even with a stiff shoulder, he still managed to fan his pistol and empty each shot into and around the silver dollar.

The next day Applejack and Bill traveled to their distant range. Once again, Jack tried drawing quickly and firing, and still he did not hit the silver dollar. Discouraged, he angrily sat down on a rock and hung his head in disgust.

Bill yelled at him.

"Quitter, are yeah? The going gets tough and you give up? Here now, holster that pistol and build a little fire. Go on! Do as I say!"

The young man reluctantly did as instructed and when he had a small fire started, Bill Smith looked on with a smirk on his hard, leathered, and deeply tanned face. Then the gunfighter kicked apart the flames. Picking up a smoking stick, charred black, he went to the cliff, and to the right of the tree began scraping a silhouette of a man. When the charcoal ran out, he repeated the process until the outline on the stone wall was complete. Bill then drew a small circle dead center in the middle of the figure—the circle being the same size as a silver dollar.

"Now," said Bill, "go ahead and shoot...just like I taught you, partner."

Slowly, Applejack stood up.

"Don't act like a mouse! Stand up like a man and put some energy into it!"

Angry, Applejack drew his revolver with a vengeance, and his first bullet hit dead center in the charcoal man's body.

"Now fan it!" said Bill. "Just like I taught you!"

The young man fanned the hammer of his newly filed pistol, and five shots echoed close together in a steady roar and struck all around the charcoal circle. Bill smiled broadly at his student's success and thumped him on the back. In awe, Applejack walked up to the cliff and examined the location of each bullet strike.

"I'd say," said Bill, "that's as close as a man can get to hitting his mark. Nearly dead center, and each one of them lead pills would have killed your man. Maybe someday you'll get as good as me and hit the dollar, but from my way of thinkin, you just graduated from the Bill Smith School of Gunfighten! Haw! Haw!"

In silence, the two men rode back to camp.

Instinctively, both knew their companionship was coming to an end.

"Kid, how come you didn't do much talking? Every youngster I ever met couldn't keep his fool mouth shut."

"I'm not as young as you think, Bill," said Applejack, "maybe in years, but not in life. I didn't want to upset you, but you talked about your Ma when you was sick. I figure you and I have the same upbringing."

"What do you mean by that, kid? Just exactly what did I say?"

"You took care of your Ma like I did. Right up to the end. I figure down deep you aren't as bad as…"

"Kid! If it wasn't you sayin those words, I'd kill you sure."

"Then maybe it would have been better if I had said nothin."

"Maybe. But now that the subject's come up, I been meanin to ask if you were going to join me."

"I've been thinkin on it," responded Applejack. "Given that my prospects aren't real bright, but…"

"But…you don't want to make the break."

"If you mean I don't want to become an outlaw; you're right. You see, I was brought up…I …"

"You made certain promises to your Ma and Pa."

"That's it."

"Son, we all got to follow our own path. As for me, I was tired of all that grubbin in the dirt and worrying about the crops and the weather, and… Heck, it don't make no never mind. When my folks died, I swore I'd never go without again."

"I know, you said as much when you were sick," said Applejack.

"Boy, you know way too much about me. The very first to know and still be breathin. Well then...this is where we part."

"I reckon."

"Just remember, Applejack," said the man who called himself Bill Smith, "a feller don't never git somethin for nothin. It's what a man is willin to pay that makes the difference in this life. As for me...I take what I want and if someone thinks he's man enough to stop me...let him try. You remember that."

"I will, Bill."

"Then good. As far as I'm concerned, we're square, kid. Next time we meet, don't ever expect no favors. You and me, for a moment, come as close as I'm ever willin to get with some feller still wet behind the ears."

"I'll remember that."

In late afternoon the two men packed up. They saddled horses, then tied down saddlebags and bedrolls. Applejack loaded a full pannier onto the mare. Getting into the saddles, it was the outlaw that spoke first.

"Well, son, I reckon I owe you my life. And I hope I made a fair trade in teachin yeah how to shoot."

"You did that, Bill, and I'm much obliged. Do you want any of these foodstuffs you bought?"

"Nawww, you keep them. Be seeing you, kid. Oh, and one more thing—that pistol of yours is a mighty delicate instrument. If I were you, when ridin, I'd leave the hammer over an empty chamber. Just for safety sake, mind you."

Chapter 4

Applejack watched as the outlaw rode south, and after a while the young man followed. When he reached Aguilar, he rode down Main Street to the cantina, dismounted, and tied both horses to posts. Entering the establishment, a slight smile crossed the cowboy's face. He saw the tough Mexican who had insulted and struck him more than a month before. He was standing at the bar. Jack took a chair and table, and when the rotund server came, he ordered the same food and drink. The expression on the bar owner's face told it all.

"Well!" shouted the Mexican bandit. "The baby gringo is back! Maybe he wants another leetle lesson!"

"That's it exactly," said Applejack, coming to his feet.

Before entering the bar, Jack had made sure to remove the leather thong from around the hammer and to load the empty chamber.

"Haw! Has the baby cowboy grown teeth?"

"Call it as you see it," responded Applejack. "But if you reach for that iron on your hip, I'll put holes in you."

Complete silence filled the bar. The brute of a man firmed his lips. Taking the thong off his pistol, he stared at the young cowboy. Slowly, his dark face began to grow a smile.

"I'm going to like this verrry much," said the bandit.

The bully began his draw and before his pistol came up, Applejack, with weeks of practice, felt the muscles of his right hand lift the .45. It nearly jumped into his grasp and fanning the hammer twice, the first bullet struck the big Mexican's rising revolver and fist. Blood and pistol flew. The second bullet hit a thigh. The Mexican shouted in pain as his leg was crumpled out from under him and he hit face first onto the hard stone floor. The big man bounced down on his head and did not move. Pools of blood were forming where the bullets had struck.

"Bring me my dinner," said Applejack to the owner while punching out empties and reloading. "When I finish and leave, you can take care of that!"

The tough hombre on the stone floor of the cantina lay there and bled while the owner scurried around the body to bring food to the young man. Applejack quickly ate part of his meal. The wounded fellow moaned and called for help. Walking out the open door and to his horses, Jack pondered the outcome of this fight. The big bully weeks earlier gave him a hard lesson in life, and now he, Applejack, had returned an even harder one. Releasing the animals and getting into the saddle, he rode out of town. Once back on the trail, he headed south towards Trinidad, another twenty some miles to go.

Was I wrong to confront the bully? thought Applejack. *How many others had the man harmed, and in that very cantina? The owner didn't seem too fond of the big Mexican. The tough would have shot and killed me, but I had no such intention. I just wanted to bring him down a notch or two. Bet I'm the first to knock the stuffings out of him in a long while. I wonder what Pa would have had to say about it. Ma for sure would scold me for going too far.*

"Bucky," said the young man to his horse. "I bet it won't change that fellow, but it ought to slow him down.

We better get moving; we got a ways to go."

Looking at his father's silver watch, he saw it was four o'clock in the afternoon and, counting on his fingers, he figured it would be midnight before he arrived.

"Hoss, should I be going into saloons or not? Where else am I going to hunt up work? Cowboying is all I know anything about. Trinidad's a busy place and a rough town. Will anybody hire me?"

The young man followed the main road toward the city. This was an ancient trail used by Indians, plainsmen, and now by an invading crowd of settlers. Hours later, the sun set behind the mountains. The night sky was like black velvet, and the stars shone brightly above. In the clear air the heavens looked close enough to reach up and touch. A half moon was rising. The brightness of stars and moon lit up the path the horses followed and created dark shadows. Coyotes hunted in packs, and they called to each other from vast distances. Occasionally rabbits eating grass beside the road ran in front or behind the horse's hooves as they passed down the trail. The heat of the day had dissipated, and the slight coolness of a faint breeze was pleasant as it passed over the cowboy's face. It was a special night in the young man's life and made him feel elated and glad to be alive.

Applejack rode past houses that skirted the edge of Trinidad. It was the biggest town he had ever seen. There were all kinds of stores and businesses with large signs advertising their wares. Some of the buildings were more than two stories and made of brick. There were houses built around Main Street going on for avenue after avenue. Even though it was midnight, there were men on the boardwalks and the bars were open. Music was playing and shouts and course laughter rang up and down the street, some from men's throats and others from the shrill upper register of females.

Applejack wondered what was to become of him. Would he be able to resist temptations and follow the teachings of his parents? Their voices and warnings repeated unwillingly in his head. Often they had told him about excessiveness in wild towns like Trinidad. They warned him of fast talking city folk; places where a man could find plenty of trouble and little good. Ringing in his head were his father's words: "Best you can do when you go to a town, is finish your business and be gone out of there." From his mother he remembered clearly what she often repeated: "Son, I expect you to live a clean life, and be a good man." Applejack rode up the street, towing the bay mare behind. Despite himself, he felt like a little kid entering a candy store.

Fascinated, Applejack pulled reins in front of the Imperial Saloon, dismounted, and tied both horses to a rail. Entering the bar, the young man was greeted with music from a small band, and fellows and saloon girls were dancing. At the rear were poker tables and a faro game. Men were talking loudly, some dressed in suits, and gambling away their month's pay. Looking up at the high ceilings and fancy hanging lights, Jack walked to the bar and, for the first time in his life, ordered a beer. He paid with a coin, took a swallow from the sudsy brew, and found that the first taste was not to his liking. Attempting to fit in, he turned and watched the patrons as he held his beer. Eventually he pulled out his father's pocket watch. The time was ten minutes to twelve. Never in his life had he been in such a fancy saloon. Under any other circumstances he would have been sound asleep in his bed at home, or lying on the ground in his bedroll after a day of hard riding and guarding cattle.

For some time Applejack stood at the bar, sipping his beer. Then, seeing an empty table, he carried the drink there and sat down. On the table was a newspaper; that day's edition. Reading papers was a rare treat for isolated Westerners. Jack picked it up, unfolded it, and read the day's date: June 28, 1882. Glancing over the headline and several articles, he found one that interested him. *"There are now two 'bankers' running for city offices—Mr. Taylor of the Las Animas County Bank, and Mr. Masterson of the bank of 'FairO' . They each have a large number of depositors, one of time depositors and the other receives his deposits for keeps."* Reading further, Applejack discovered that it was Bat Masterson, town marshal, who was being ridiculed for being a gambler and a faro dealer on the side.

Everybody in the West had heard of Bat Masterson, the famous former sheriff, lawman, and US Deputy Marshal. People knew he was friends with Wyatt Earp and Doc Holliday. Why, even had Jack heard, back on his parent's homestead, about Masterson and how he practiced shooting all the time, was a crack shot, and that no outlaw would face him in a fair fight. Applejack even heard that the lawman liked his drink. There was a story going around that the marshal, irritated by city officials, occasionally got drunk and would stagger down Trinidad's Main Street late in the evening and shoot out street lights. Then, later, he would make amends by paying for the damages.

Looking to the back of the bar and the faro game,

Applejack wondered if that was Bat Masterson himself standing as banker and running the dealing box. The young man didn't know much about the world, but occasional papers came to his parent's homestead, where they would devour every word. Whenever a story about gambling arose, his father would warn him about throwing his money away. His father would say, "It's a wicked world out there, Jack. You be best to stay out of them towns and do your chores. Idle hands are the devil's workshop."

Occasionally a hired hand would be brought home or a wanderer would stop at the hardscrabble ranch, and they would stay for a night or until the work was done. Applejack would take every opportunity to ask questions and learn all he could about the outside world. This is where he learned about faro and gathered a modicum of knowledge of how the game works. Ever since, Jack was itching to try to play at least one game, but losing even a couple of dollars was more than he could afford.

Applejack got up and, taking his full beer with him, he turned in the direction of the faro table. Then he remembered the newspaper, an item he seldom came across. Putting the beer down, he picked up the paper, easily folded it into a small rectangle, and stuffed it into his jacket pocket. Picking up his drink, he headed for the green baize table.

There was one man playing faro, and his expression was intense as he swayed back and forth, laying his money down, making his bet, and losing.

"Masterson, you scoundrel! That box is loaded and you're cheating!"

"Bob, we're both in our drink, and it would be a

mistake for us to continue," responded the dealer. "Suppose we end the game now and let me close up, before we both do something we regret."

While the faro dealer was speaking, Applejack saw the man named Bob draw a revolver from underneath his coat with his left hand and hold it tight against his pant leg. When the dealer looked down, Bob raised his weapon and Applejack stepped close, his pistol in hand, and chopped the wrist of the angry and drunken gambler. The man's heavy .45 revolver clattered loudly across the floor. The faro dealer extricated himself from the table, walked to where the pistol lay, and picked it up.

"Ohh," exclaimed Bob. "You broke my wrist!"

Raising a right fist, the drunken gambler swung and the young man ducked, still holding his full glass of beer. So far, none of it had spilled. The dealer came up behind Bob and struck him hard with his own weapon. The fellow went limp and folded to the floor.

"Thank you, young man," said the faro dealer, putting out his right hand. "My name's Bat Masterson. I'm in your debt."

Applejack stuck out his hand and noted the slight sway of the lawman. He was indeed in his cups, although his speech was not slurred.

"Folks call me Applejack, and it's my pleasure, sir," said the young man, shaking Masterson's hand.

"Give me a minute to close down the table and give the dealer box and money to the bartender. I'll get someone to take care of Bob. I'm afraid the drink affected his judgment. If he didn't want to lose, he shouldn't have played. It's as simple as that."

Applejack set his beer on a table. Masterson took

money and the dealer box to the bar, spoke to several men standing there, and said his goodbyes. Swaying a bit, he returned to where the young cowboy was standing.

"I haven't seen you before, Jack. New to town?"

"I just rode in. Matter of fact, my horses are outside."

"Horses?"

"Yes, my pack horse with supplies and my…"

"Planning on staying long?"

"Yeah, if I can find work."

"Have a job lined up?" asked Masterson.

"Not yet, sir, but…"

"I'll tell you what, meet me here tomorrow at noon and we'll go for a ride and have a talk. Can you do that?"

"Yes sir, I have nothing to…"

"Good!" exclaimed the town marshal. "I'll see you then."

Applejack followed Masterson through the open saloon doors and onto the boardwalk. The marshal walked briskly, if not a little unsteadily, around a corner and disappeared. Going to his mount, the young westerner untied the reins of both horses.

"Well, Bucky," whispered Applejack to his horse, "things might be looking up. Can you believe it, old friend? That was Bat Masterson, himself."

Taking reins and walking down the street, he headed for the nearest stable. It took some time, but he finally woke the hostler and made payment. Applejack helped remove tack and supplies and stable the horses. Paying two bits, he hung his saddle and bridle on a rail and took his gear up to the loft. There he found a spot to lay out his bedroll. Lying down, he listened to the breathing and rustling of the animals below and speculated just what

Marshal Masterson would want with the likes of him. It took some time before the excitement of the day allowed him to drift off to sleep.

It was a rooster crowing that woke Applejack. He left his gear in the loft (except his new pistol, which he tucked in his belt) and climbed down. Out back, he found a pump and water trough. There was a little mirror, soap, and a towel. Jack removed his shirt, soaped himself down, and rinsed under the pump. The water was cold but refreshing. He combed his wet hair and then, breaking a twig from an apple tree, he chewed on the soft wood and used it as a brush to scrub his white teeth. It was something his mother demanded of him since he was a child. Her words rang in his ears, "Cleanliness is next to Godliness." Habit was a demanding master.

An hour later, the hostler awoke and came out of his small quarters in the back. He made his way to the pump; not to wash, but to get a drink and fill his coffee pot.

"You're up early, lad," said the old man.

"Morning," replied Applejack, stepping back from the bearded and odiferous fellow.

"Find the hay loft to your liking?"

"Softer than sleeping on the ground."

"I see you found the soap and towel. Ambitious of you. Now me, I wash when the mood strikes me. Working in a stable, one seems to lose…"

"Is it alright if I stay in the loft a few more nights? Until I…"

"Suit yourself, but it's one bit a night for you and two bits for the hosses."

"Can you tell me where I can get breakfast?"

"Pricey or cheap?"

"Cheap."

"Down this side street to the end. There's the Alpine. Carlos runs it. If you don't mind hot sauce with your eggs."

"Thanks."

Applejack followed the directions and found the eatery. It was clean enough, and the food was tasty and inexpensive.

The homeless and unemployed young man spent the morning washing down and currying his horses. The hostler came out and lifted a hoof on each one.

"I thought so; they both need trimming and new shoes."

"How much?" asked Jack.

"The blacksmith is a friend of mine, so it depends."

"It'll have to wait," replied Jack. "I need a job first."

"You can't wait too long. Say, if youse are lookin for work, I can always use a hand cleaning stables. Can't pay more than two bits a day and board for you. The hosses would have to stay in the corral out back. I'd be mighty obliged, if..."

"Thanks, I'll think on it," said Jack. "But I'm meeting a fellow at noon..."

"Aww, that's the way of it. I just can't seem to find no decent help. Well...on with you lad, I got to do some serious mucking."

Too nervous to lay down, Applejack went to the loft and retrieved his holster. He strapped it on and climbed down. Going to Bucky's stall, he bridled and saddled the horse himself and walked him down an ally and to Main Street. By his father's watch, he was a half-hour early. He tied his mount to a rail and went into the Imperial.

He'd learned his lesson and ordered what he liked: a nice cool sarsaparilla. Even though it was noon, the bar was crowded and Jack was lost among the patrons. Some were Hispanic in various forms of dress, and there were businessman, foreigners just off the train, and cowhands. It made for a noisy crowd.

At exactly noon, Bat Masterson walked through the open door. He stopped to let his vision adjust to the darkness of the bar. Patrons looked up, noted the marshal's presence, and the saloon quieted. Applejack approached warily, wondering if the lawman would actually recall last night's encounter.

"Applejack, if I remember correctly?" said Masterson, offering his right hand.

The young cowboy reached out and shook it.

"Yes, sir, it's good to see you again."

"Thought I was too far in my cups, did you? Well... I was a bit..."

"Sir, I just wondered if you were still willing to meet me."

"I'm here, aren't I? And having time to review the situation, I do believe, young man, that I am indebted to you. The way I see it, you might have saved my life. Not that we want this to get around, me being the town marshal and all."

"No, sir!"

"Well, are you ready?"

"Sir?"

"Call me marshal or Mr. Masterson, no need to be too formal. What I meant is, are you ready for a ride?"

"Yes, marshal. I have my horse out front."

"Good, just follow me to the bar. I had a couple gunny

sacks made up and between the two of us, we'll each carry one."

The lawman took a loaded gunny sack from the bartender and handed it to Jack. There was a slight clinking of glass and, feeling the side of the bag, the cowboy surmised they were empty liquor bottles. Masterson took the other sack and led the way out of the bar. It was a little awkward, but both men managed to untie reins and mount, the bulky sacks resting across the pommels. The lawman turned and headed out of town, south and toward Raton Pass.

Applejack followed. Because of the bottles, the marshal walked his horse and the young man did the same, wondering just what Masterson had in mind. It wasn't difficult to assume that some target practice was the goal, but why was he being brought along?

Once out of Trinidad, the horses had to climb. They ascended the lower part of the mountain and turned off the trail and into a cul-de-sac. Applejack found they were surrounded by a U-shaped wall of rock. Dismounting, the marshal took his burden of bottles and carried it to a ledge of rock. He untied the gunny sack and began placing the tall empty glass containers a foot apart along a stone bench. Without saying a word, Masterson nodded his head, indicating that Applejack should follow his example. Glass fragments lay on the bench and across the ground. Pieces crunched under the young man's boots. Jack copied the marshal's movements. When the task was completed, they went back to the horses.

"Once, I only hobbled my horse," said Masterson. "When I began shooting, the fool horse still managed to get away. So, I learned to use a rope as well. I suggest you do the same." Both men worked at securing their mounts.

Wondering what would be accomplished by shooting at bottles, the young cowboy waited for what would come next. Certainly the marshal wasn't there to give him a shooting lesson.

Masterson laid out a box of ammunition on a rock and loaded a sixth bullet into an empty chamber of his pistol.

"Despite being in my drink," said the marshal, "I saw that you made a decision and acted quickly when Bob tried to sneak a shot at me. Most men would have been slower, or not acted at all. I wanted to see if my guess was right or not. Can you use that Colt of yours?"

With steady hand the lawman calmly raised his arm straight and fired. The furthest whisky bottle to the right blew up in a shattering of glass. It appeared to be hit dead center. The noise was deafening and the horses side-stepped and Bucky neighed in annoyance.

"I never get tired of that," said Masterson. "It gives instant satisfaction, and there's something about the breaking of the glass. Your turn."

Applejack undid the leather strap to the hammer, hesitated, then made a lightning draw. He fired at the second bottle, and missed. The bullet hit rock further on against the canyon wall and ricocheted. Once again the horse hooves sounded in agitation.

"No," said the marshal. "Not a fast draw. Just aim and shoot. I want to see if you can hit the target. It's important in my line of business. Now do it the way I did."

This time, Applejack raised his arm, aimed and fired at the same bottle, and once again he missed. Perturbed, Bat

Masterson raised his revolver and as quickly as he aimed, he shot five bottles in succession, each one hit dead center and exploding into small pieces.

"I guess I was wrong about you, Jack," said Masterson. "Let's see if you can hit any of those bottles. The way you shoot, I would guess you can hit one out of five. In the law business, that's just not good enough."

"That's right Marshal Masterson," said Jack. "Back on my father's ranch, when I went potting at rabbits, it was one out of five. But a month ago, I helped a feller out. He was wounded in the shoulder and I patched him up. In return, while he was healing, he offered to teach me how to shoot."

"Looks to me that he didn't do a very good..."

"He taught the point and shoot method," said Applejack.

"Doesn't look like..."

"Here, let me show you."

Applejack walked through an opening in the bench of stone where the bottles stood, and up to a solid wall of rock. Bending down, he picked up a chalky-looking rock and began drawing an image. Soon, it took on the crude shape of a human figure. When the picture was completed the faint outline of a westerner lay sketched on the stone. Looking at his work, Jack moved forward and added a small circle, dead center and about the size of a silver dollar.

Going back to where Masterson stood, Jack drew his pistol, pulled back the gate, spun the cylinder and emptied two spent cartridges. Then he pulled three bullets from his belt and filled the empty spaces. Closing the gate, he holstered his pistol. Looking over at the lawman, Applejack stuck out his tongue and wet dry lips.

"Well...that was dramatic," commented the marshal. "Go ahead, show me this point and shoot method. I'm interested."

"I'm a bit nervous, sir. I mean..."

"That's the whole point of bringing you here, Jack. When a man's shooting back, one is bound to be a whole lot more nervous than what I can make you. Now, shoot!"

Applejack felt the same anger rising in him that Bill Smith had provoked just some days ago. Moving his hand down to the butt of his revolver, the muscles reflexed into long-practiced action. As fast as Jack could fan and pull the trigger, the six heavy pellets of lead struck into the carved figure on the wall. The repeated explosions sounded a deafening and continuous roar. Behind, both horses screamed and raised up on rear hooves. If it wasn't for the ropes tied around their necks and to a tree, they would have run away.

"Well...I'll be," said Masterson, and then he let out a long low whistle.

As he was taught, Applejack began punching out empties and replaced the chambers with six live bullets from his belt. The lawman saw that and smiled. Then the young man followed as Masterson walked to the wall and began examining the bullet strikes. Only one had hit the center circle, but five others were placed very near it.

"Good shooting, kid," said the lawman. "Now tell me, just who taught you this?"

"He told me to call him Bill Smith."

"He did, huh? You say he was shot and you fixed him up? By any chance, did he let on how he made a living?"

"By taking," said Applejack. "He invited me to join him, but I told him I couldn't. He said we were even and the next time I met him, not to expect to be given any breaks."

"Describe him," said Masterson.

Applejack did his best to recall the man's features.

"Sounds like the outlaw Bill Peacock. He's deadly with a pistol and I wouldn't want to tangle with him. You were lucky the man took a liking to you.

"I didn't say that," replied Jack.

"Well...if he hadn't, you'd be dead. Take my word for it."

"Yes, sir."

"I told you to call me marshal or Mr. Masterson, kid. Now I'll explain why I brought you out here. When I was asked to come to Trinidad to be the law, I brought my own men with me. One I lost over a drunken gunfight, and one quit. I'm in need of men with nerve, who can think and shoot. I won't say you always hit what you aim at, but you sure can put lead where it's needed. My offer is thirty a month, take it or leave it."

"You want me?"

"I asked, didn't I? Just do what I say, and we'll get along fine. But you should know the job might not last long. Some people seem a might upset with my outside gambling...and heck...I do like my drink. Life's too short, and if I can't enjoy myself, what's the use? What I'm saying is, there's a chance I'll be voted out of office. Until then, you got a job."

"I don't know what to say," replied Jack.

"Say, yes. I'm paying you out of my own pocket. What they provide me each month doesn't even cover my expenses. That's why I do business on the side."

"Maybe you should pay me less, marshal."

"No, thirty a month is fair for putting your life on the line. But, there shouldn't be too much danger. When we got here, Trinidad was one of the roughest towns in the West. It's calmed down considerable. Run out of office or not, when we leave, it'll be a peaceful place. I guarantee that."

"Mr. Masterson, I'd be mighty pleased to work for you."

"Well then, let's knock down the rest of these bottles and get back to town. I want you working the night shift, and I'll give you instructions."

The sound of gunfire echoed off the canyon walls and then stopped. A group of travelers, taking wagons over the pass, watched as two horses and riders came out of a rock canyon and turned north down the mountain towards Trinidad.

Chapter 5

Applejack discovered that his father wasn't the only tough man. Bat Masterson had a hard and seasoned crew of deputies. He expected them to show up for work on time, be prepared to do the job, and do exactly as told. The town marshal didn't permit gun-play unless a lawman was fired upon first. A deputy couldn't fire back if people were standing in the way, but must protect himself by getting out of the line of fire. Roughing up a prisoner was forbidden, but if a drunk was a danger to himself and others, a good clout on the head with a pistol barrel was the most efficient method of subduing a prisoner.

"I don't want any of you hurt," said the marshal. "It was a drunk who killed my brother Ed, and I don't want to lose another man like I lost him. Don't fool with a drunk. If he gives you trouble, thump him good and drag him off to jail."

Masterson expected a routine to be followed. Doors were checked at night, and patrolling the saloons and business district was a must. All toughs and rough characters were disarmed when in Trinidad, and that element knew that Bat Masterson was not someone to mess with. Under the marshal's leadership, the criminals kept away and many moved to other more lawless towns.

Applejack found he was teased by the other deputies for being so green. The fact that he didn't drink or smoke and had little experience with the rawer side of life led to endless pranks or jokes. Most of that stopped when the men gathered for shooting practice, which was required by Masterson.

"He's the first deputy I hired that has a different way of shooting," said the marshal, "but he's a fellow I'd hate to go up against. I'm convinced he would drop me before I got my revolver half way out of my holster."

Applejack survived a month by keeping his mouth shut and performing his duty with the man he was assigned. Masterson wanted his men to patrol with another deputy and the system worked well. Jack's partner went by the name of Smitty, and he was a tough character who swore frequently, drank to excess, and was very good with a revolver. He was a longstanding friend of Masterson, first meeting him when hide hunting and killing buffalo, years before.

Smitty teased his young partner relentlessly.

"You vex me, Jack," said the older lawman.

"How's that?"

"What Masterson sees in a namby-pamby like you, has got me…"

"Keep it up," replied the young deputy, "and you can take off those guns, and we'll see who's…"

"So you've been saying."

"This morning, after our shift, meet me behind the Imperial, and I'll try my best to make you see my point of view," said Applejack.

"Masterson doesn't like fighting between…"

"He doesn't like cowards, either. Shall I tell him…"

"Alright, Jack. I was just kidding. But who can respect a feller who doesn't drink or consort with women?"

"Smitty, I've had enough. Keep it up and next target

practice, I'll call you out; and it won't be with fists."

"Alright, alright, Jack. Everyone knows you're fast. Just don't act so high and mighty, and we'll get along."

"I'm not acting anything, Smitty. Take me as I am, or leave me alone."

"See? You can't even swear, can you? The phrase is, 'or leave me the hell alone.'"

Chapter 6

Masterson's deputies patrolled the city day and night. It was amazing how, in one short year, Trinidad, one of the most lawless towns in the west, settled down to being a safer place to live. It was all the doing of Bat Masterson, the deputies he brought with him, and his seasoned skill as a lawman. It bewildered Applejack that the town's people could be so disloyal. To actually want to vote for someone else other than Masterson seemed ridiculous. All because the marshal liked to drink and doubled as a faro dealer.

Morality is hard taskmaster, thought Applejack one evening as he heard businessmen talk when closing their shops. *Hypocrites, that's the word for it. No other lawman has accomplished what Masterson has done*

Unlike his fellow deputies, when Applejack entered bars, he did not drink or spend his money. On Sundays he attended the Catholic Church, and from the very first he became infatuated with a young woman; one who always sat in the same pew with her family. Perhaps someday he would have the opportunity to meet her. Jack was not sure the position as deputy would be in the family's favor, and besides, he had nothing to offer.

Each Sunday he exited the church, always managing to time his departure behind the girl and her family. On one occasion he had caught her interest, and each Sunday after, she had returned his nod and smile. It was an odd way to court a young woman, but somehow Applejack would find a way to meet her.

It was on one such Sunday that a group of deputies attended a celebration after church. It was an outside picnic. Food was served on plank tables. Chairs and benches were arranged behind the church, musicians strummed their instruments, and couples danced. It was the opportunity Applejack was looking for. When the girl's parents got up to dance, Jack approached.

"I have been wanting to meet you."

"Please, señor! We have not been introduced."

"Is this feller bothering you, lady?" asked Smitty.

Behind the lawman were three more of the town deputies, most in their drink despite it being early afternoon.

"Smitty," said Applejack. "This is not the time or the place. I beg of you, let us alone."

"So, all of a sudden you've become a ladies' man?" said the troublemaker, shoving Jack.

The other deputies laughed. A crowd of churchgoers looked on at the commotion of the drunken men. Angered beyond measure for the first time in his life, Applejack lashed out and struck Smitty a terrific blow. It was a right fist to the chin and the man went down, knocked out cold. Other deputy marshals confronted Applejack and he found himself in a fistfight with three of his fellows. In a moment, Jack was getting the worst of it.

By then the music had stopped. The girl retreated and was standing with her parents. The parishioners watched as a table of food was turned over while the four men struggled. To all appearances, the celebration was ruined. Then, out of the crowd stepped Bat Masterson. His deputies stopped the altercation with Applejack and came to stand in great dread before their boss.

"Get out of here," ordered the marshal. "I'll attend to you three later. Take Smitty with you."

The three deputies picked up the unconscious man, and they carried him away from the crowd and down the street.

"What's this about, Jack?" asked Masterson.

"I was speaking to her," Applejack said, pointing, "and Smitty interfered. He's been after me ever since I first..."

"I know, and I was going to see how you handled it. I'd say you won the argument. Smitty's fired, and I'm keeping you, Jack. Now let's see if we can..."

The priest walked through the crowd and stopped before the two law officers.

"Thank you, Marshal Masterson," said the priest, "but I am afraid your intervention is a little late. I saw what happened from the church steps, and it pains me to say your law keepers started this."

"I know, and I apologize. I will pay for the damages. Would a hundred help improve the situation?" asked Masterson, taking a bill from a pocket and handing it to the priest.

"I was not asking for money, but for what the town's people are desiring: a little restraint and discipline from you and your men."

"That hurts, but I see your point of view, Father. Please keep the money as a donation. But speaking on behalf of my new deputy, Applejack: as you can see, he was merely protecting a young girl's honor."

"Perhaps, but for the moment, I think it would be best if both of you..."

"Certainly, Father, we will go. But please don't let this reflect on Jack. He's one of my best men, and he doesn't drink. Tell your parishioners we apologize, but remember that when we came here, this was a lawless town. It took equally tough men to tame it. I will do my best to see this won't happen again."

Masterson took Applejack's arm and, noticing blood trickling from a large gash on his deputy's face, gave him a handkerchief.

"Come, Jack. I think in this case, 'discretion is the better part of valor.'"

The congregation watched as the marshal and his deputy left the churchyard and disappeared up the street.

"Maria!" exclaimed Alfonso Martinez, the girl's father. "We are going home and perhaps you can explain in private why that…that…gunman was speaking to you! You have made a spectacle of our family!"

Chapter 7

A month passed and Applejack continued to attend the church, but the parishioners made it a point to ignore him. Maria was guarded by her father, mother, and other relatives, and the young admirer could not get close; not even when she was leaving Mass. Then, one afternoon after service, the priest came and talked to the deputy sitting out on the steps of the church.

"Young man," began the priest, "I admire your perseverance. Most men would have given up by now. I am afraid that as a lawman for Marshal Masterson, you are not popular with the Spanish people. I know what I am talking about, having similar difficulties, being a priest from Holland and not speaking Spanish myself."

"Why aren't we popular? Because we keep the law?" asked Applejack.

"Perhaps it is the vigor by which you keep it."

"We only arrest the ones who have created trouble."

"But you must understand that before white men came, this was a Spanish town, with Spanish lawmen. They have their own traditions. Many of these people resent change."

"Maybe it doesn't matter. The way I hear it, Masterson will be voted out of office."

"And then you and his deputies will go with him?"

"Maybe. I didn't take this job out of choice, but because it was the only one offered to me."

"And, if you had a choice?"

"I would pick out a little ranch with plenty of water and raise cattle and horses. One that would keep a family and make a little extra."

"Plenty of water is a hard ranch to find in this country. And one as young as you would be hard-pressed to..."

"Yes, Father. I left my parents' homestead after they died. It just didn't have the grass or water, and it was not worth keeping."

"My name is Father Munnecom, and you are Jack Martin?"

"My friends call me Applejack," the young man said, shaking the priest's hand.

"Suppose you come to the rectory and we sit down over a cup of coffee. Since your interest in Maria Martinez doesn't seem to lessen, I would like to get to know you better. Already, I can tell you are not at all like Mr. Masterson's other deputies."

"No, Father, I guess I'm not."

Applejack followed the priest into his private quarters. They sat at a table. The housekeeper served coffee and biscuits. For over an hour they talked.

"Applejack," said the priest, "I find your views interesting. I see that you have lived a rather isolated life on your parents' ranch, yet I believe they have taught you well. Obviously, your mother was educated, and it seems you have read books she provided you. There are many young men born and raised here who cannot read at all. And, you have taken to heart what your parents have taught you. For your age, you are a very moral young man. Suppose we continue our conversations?"

"Thank you, Father. I enjoyed speaking with you; but to what end would further talk..."

"You do want to meet and, shall we say, court Maria Martinez?"

"Yes, of course."

"Then you must be formally introduced to the parents, and you must follow their Spanish traditions. Then again, as a suitor you must have something to offer..."

"I can't offer anything..."

"Precisely, Jack. Next Sunday—not after church, but say at four in the afternoon—come knocking on my door, and I will be here waiting. Perhaps, between the two of us, we can find ways to advance your cause."

Applejack stood to go, and he shook the priest's hand.

"Thank you, Father. I will be here at four as you request. But still, I don't see..."

"Everyone in this life needs a friend," replied Father Munnecom, "and I think, young man, that you will find I make a good one. In the meantime, I will lend you a book. It is a favorite of mine, and I think it will provide much entertainment. Are you familiar with Alexandre Dumas? No? Try reading this. It is called, *The Count of Monte Cristo*. It is about intrigue and revenge. I highly recommend it."

Applejack found himself outside and alone on the steps of the rectory. Somewhat bewildered by the kindness of the older man, Jack walked towards his meager shack on the other side of town, book in hand.

Chapter 8

Father Munnecom rang a bell. Jemina, his housekeeper, came, and the priest ordered more coffee and a sandwich. When the food arrived, he closed and locked the door to his study.

Alfonso Martinez, thought the priest. *You have been a thorn in my side ever since I arrived. You have tried to thwart my every move with your money and your arrogance. Several times you purchased land out from under me; good investments lost. But you couldn't stop me from buying that cantina and setting up gambling. I have been looking for a way to get back at you, and I am willing to wager that Applejack might be that path. Just think, Alfonso: your daughter marrying a gringo, mixing your proud Spanish blood with a common cowboy.*

The priest drank his coffee and ate his sandwich, then carefully cut off one end of a cigar and lit it. From a locked desk drawer, he took a bottle of whiskey and poured two fingers into a glass. Such American anachronisms amused the man of cloth.

Two fingers, indeed! This Trinidad, this United States of America! If I am to remain in this uncultured country, I will profit by it. Yes, God, I will do your work, but when I go back to Holland and my Europe, I will do it as a rich man. 'Applejack', what an amusing name. Boy, I have taken a liking to you, and I will help you to further both our ends. If I will teach you anything, you will learn that people are not always what they seem; not me or even your precious and sheltered Maria. Life, my dear naïve Jack, has a way of changing people, and you will find that out, soon enough.

Chapter 9

A half moon was up, but very bright; and along with the stars made enough light to create shadows. It was three in the morning, and Applejack was patrolling with a new partner named Flint.

Jack and Flint heard a gunshot from another street. Both men left their scheduled patrol and ran toward the sound. This shooting so early in the morning was ominous. When the next shot rang out, Applejack recognized it as coming from a revolver. A third explosion, and then a fourth, echoed down the street, and he continued running. Turning onto the Main Street of town, the two deputies heard a fifth shot and saw glass shards fly from the force of a bullet. A streetlight flickered and then went out. Slowing, they came upon a dark figure dressed in a suit and wearing a bowler hat. Before them, walking in a forced but somewhat staggering condition, was their boss, Trinidad's elected police officer Marshal Bat Masterson.

Applejack was first to reach him. Masterson raised his arm, pistol in hand, and aimed at another street lamp. His young protégé grabbed the arm and prevented his boss from firing.

"What? Who would...oh...it's you, Jack," said the drunken man, looking over his shoulder.

"See! Haven't missed a target: five shots, and five lamps hit—one more to go!"

"Marshal," said Applejack. "It's three in the morning,

and you're disturbing the peace and destroying public…"

"Why, you young buck!" said Masterson, turning and swaying. "You give me orders?"

Flint came up and joined the altercation. Hesitating a few feet away, he watched the exchange between his inebriated boss and the younger deputy.

"Yes sir, in this case I am," said Applejack.

"Don't sir me!" shouted Masterson. "I told you! It's either Marshal Masterson or…"

"Boss," said Applejack, "you told us yourself that if this should happen, to stop you."

"I did?" asked Masterson, turning and looking at the young man and then waving his loaded pistol with the one live shell in front of Applejack's face. "We clean up this town for those mealy-mouthed folks and what do they want? They want to get rid of the lot of us. Just 'cause I gamble and earn some money on the side."

"You're in your cups, boss," said Applejack. "You're right, Trinidad folk should be grateful; but this isn't helping, sir."

"There you go again!" complained Masterson. "Using that word. If Earp and Doc Holliday were here, they'd show these milksops a thing or two. Watch this, Jack! Watch me shoot out the next lamp. Drunk or sober, I never miss!"

Somehow, Bat Masterson jerked his arm free, and he began to aim for a sixth street lamp, its flame flickering brightly under glass.

"Help me, Flint," said the young deputy.

His partner hesitated once again, and then moved in and grabbed the gun arm. With surprising strength and agility, Masterson jerked his gun hand free and struck the barrel across Flint's forehead. The deputy fell, out cold from the swift blow. Applejack grabbed hold of his boss and found the older man was much stronger than he expected. Masterson once again struck out with his pistol, and it came down heavily on the younger man's left shoulder. The blow hurt. Wasting no time, Applejack removed his sombrero and, placing his pistol inside the hat, struck down hard on the back of his boss's head. The marshal froze from the blow, and then started to fall. Jack caught Masterson from behind and gently lowered him to the ground.

Flint gained consciousness and looked over in time to see Applejack deliver the blow.

"I'd say," said Flint rubbing his bleeding head. "I sure wouldn't want to be you, tomorrow."

"If he even remembers," said Applejack.

"That's Bat Masterson you're talking about," replied Flint. "Drunk or not, young Jack, you can bet your life this old bull will remember every detail."

"Well...I had no choice," said Applejack. "You were out cold and he was too strong for me, so I did what he told us to do when handling a drunk."

Holding a bandanna to his bleeding forehead, Flint laughed.

"You have a point, Jack, but I still wouldn't want to be you in the morning."

Together, the two men lifted and carried the heavy man off the street and to the marshal's office. Laying Masterson on a cot in the back room, Applejack himself took a key and locked the lawman in.

"Flint, after our shift, I'll come back and take care of him. I'd appreciate it if you say nothing about this."

"Are you kidding? I value my job and my life. On that, you have my word."

In the morning, after their patrol was over, they were relieved by two deputies. Their replacements started their rounds and Flint left. Taking a key, Applejack unlocked the door and there lay his boss, out cold and snoring away. It wasn't until eleven-thirty when the marshal began to awaken. The young deputy was there, sitting in a chair. A glass and pitcher of water sat on a small table beside him.

"Jack!" said Bat Masterson, attempting to rise and then grabbing at his forehead with his right hand. "Oh, my aching head! What am I doing here?"

"Well, sir, you were in your..."

There was a long silence, and during that time, Masterson slowly managed to sit up and put his feet over the edge of the cot and onto the floor.

"Give me a drink of that water and..."

"Here is some headache powder," said the young man.

Bat Masterson took the glass, swallowed some water, dumped the powder into the glass, and drank the rest down.

"Now hold on, I'm beginning to..."

This was the moment Applejack most regretted, and whichever way it went, the young man steeled himself for what was coming next.

"Jack! You manhandled me!"

"That I did."

"Treated me like any common drunk!"

"Nothing common about it, sir, but I tried to soften the blow."

"There's that word again!"

"Marshal Masterson, you were out of control and stronger than me. You knocked out Flint, so I…"

"Jack! You struck me!"

Feeling the back of his head, the lawman touched a lump, and it was tender. He winced and then eyed Applejack, and the look he gave him was not pleasant.

"I'll pack my things and get out of Trinidad."

"Oh, you will, will you?"

"Yes, sir."

"Well, you don't get off that easy! Sit there and let me think. If you got it, give me more headache powder and water."

Prepared, Jack did as he was told.

"You wouldn't have any ice? I reckon not. You sat there all morning?"

"Yes, ah, Marshal Masterson."

"Well, at least that's something. Where's Flint? Is he alright?"

"Yes, Marshal."

"Did he, will he say…"

"He told me he wants to keep his job and his life, and he won't be telling anyone anything. His exact words, sir."

"He better not, if he knows what's good for him! Now as for you, my young…heck…I don't know what to call you."

"You told me to stop you, and that's what I did."

Masterson made two attempts to stand, and on the third, he made it. Holding his head, he began to pace, slowly at first and then faster. Staring at Applejack, his scowl changed to a frown and then to a slight smile. Surprisingly, the lawman began to laugh.

"Oww," said Masterson. "Even laughing hurts. Well, Applejack, you're a lucky man. Anyone else and I would have called him out and shot him full of holes."

"You could have tried, sir," replied Applejack.

Masterson laughed, and once again he grabbed his head.

"Well, you got a point there, don't you? The very reason I hired you. The one man who can draw faster than me and hit what he's aiming at. Or at least, close enough to it. Let me think. You go on now and get some sleep. Forget your shift, take the night off. Tomorrow at noon, meet me at the Imperial Saloon. I have a new assignment for you."

Applejack rose, went to the door, and turned.

"Is this because of last night, sir?" asked Applejack.

"No boy," said Masterson. "It's because you're the fastest gunman I have, and the man I'm sending you after is just as fast. So you won't wonder, I'm hooking you up with Kreeger, on special assignment with the Sheriff Department."

"Isn't Kreeger the one running against you for town marshal?"

"True, but I can work with any lawman to get the job done. Get a good night's sleep, because you will sure need it."

All the way back to his meager quarters, Applejack wondered why he would be working with the sheriff's department. Then he thought, *It isn't that hard to guess. It is common knowledge that Las Animas County has a violent past. Every lawman in Trinidad knows it. Bat Masterson told me that back in '72, Sheriff Tafoya was shot and killed in a dispute between three brothers. After that, Sheriff Witt was appointed to replace Tafoya. Masterson didn't seem to know much about him, or didn't want to say.*

Before Kreeger came to town, Uncle Dick Wootton was sheriff. That man really had a history! He had been a plainsman for most of his life. Only a person like him had the skills to convince a tribe of Utes to help build a road from Trinidad over Raton Pass. It was the building of that pass that makes Trinidad so difficult for us to police. Wagon trains by the hundreds crowd the town, buying supplies. With all those strangers and wagons milling about, it causes conflict with the town residents— and even between the city marshal's office and the sheriff's department. Just this year, before I was hired, Undersheriff McGraw and Trinidad's law officer George Goodell shot it out in Jaffa's Opera House. McGraw died.

Yes, they are short of lawmen.

Applejack arrived at his shack and went behind it to the barn. There he watered Bucky and the mare, and fed them hay. Still thinking about why Masterson wanted to lend him out, the young lawman tried his best to recall what more had been said. If he was going to get along with Kreeger, he must be cautious and act appropriately. From what he'd heard, there would be no second chances in dealing with that man.

I understand why the sheriff's department is shorthanded. But Masterson wants me to be with a man who rode with Quantrell and campaigned with Frank and Jessie James? Or who shot down the gunman Rice Brown in front of everyone on Main Street? Can any man work with such a killer?

Getting to his cabin, Jack went over last night's events. Fixing himself a late breakfast, he sat up for the remainder of the day. Unable to rest, he put his nose in a book, and it was late before he was able to sleep.

When he awoke, it was early morning and still dark outside. Applejack was too apprehensive about his meeting at noon to go back to sleep. Instead, he got up and fixed coffee and nibbled on a hard biscuit. Feeling grubby, he heated water on the stove, washed up, brushed his teeth, and put on fresh clothes. If he was going to meet the gunman, Sheriff Louis Kreeger, it would be in a clean set of duds and as confident a look as he could muster. After all, he was only twenty-one and had never killed a man in his life. Shot one up, maybe, but nothing beyond that. Applejack wondered if he was up to the task Masterson was assigning him.

The walk from the shack to downtown was one of the longest Applejack had taken in his life. Working with Kreeger was the last thing he wanted to do. His parents never thought much of a man who killed, no matter what the reason. Hearing Masterson go on about his past escapades and those of Wyatt Earp and Doc Holliday would make any young man wonder what the right path was. His Ma and Pa had warned him about getting mixed up with slick folk. And from what he'd heard, Kreeger was as slick as any man that ever lived, on either side of the law. What was Masterson getting him into?

Applejack was never late, but today his hesitancy made him right on time. Kreeger and Masterson were both sitting at a table in the Imperial and as clocks chimed noon, Deputy Marshal Applejack Martin entered the noisy saloon. He found his way forward and up to their table. Both men had a drink before them. A bartender came by and the young man ordered sarsaparilla.

Neither men rose, and Applejack remained standing.

"Jack," said Masterson, "meet Kreeger."

The young deputy extended arm and hand across the table to the rough-looking lawman. Kreeger just looked up. Applejack lowered his hand and remained standing.

"He looks like a kid, and green behind the ears. And he ordered a kid's drink. Now that I might be running for your office, you're not trying to make a fool out of me?"

"Kreeger," said Masterson. "Don't insult my deputy, your life might depend on it. There's not another man alive that can face down Bill Peacock; not even you."

"What makes you so sure of that?" asked Kreeger.

"Because old Bill himself taught this kid how to shoot. Applejack is the fastest I've ever seen and hits his mark every time. You got my word on it."

"Well, boy," said Kreeger, "if that's true, don't stand there like a lost puppy; pull up a chair and sit down."

Applejack did as he was told, and at the same time the bartender brought his drink.

"Don't let these law-dogs antagonize you, kid," said the bartender, smiling. "I got a sweet tooth myself and would rather down one of these than that hard liquor they're drinking."

Applejack kept his mouth shut and after some talk about horse racing, gambling, and fist fighting, Bat Masterson started to explain, in as low a voice as he could, why his deputy was teaming up with Kreeger.

"Bill Peacock has formed a new gang, and they're hitting merchants in the county, relieving travelers of their money and robbing a wagon or two. It's time to stop him. He's giving Trinidad, the sheriff's department, and all lawmen a bad name. Applejack, you follow Kreeger's lead and track down Peacock and his men. Don't come back until…"

"I befriended Bill," said Applejack. "I'm not sure…"

"Given what happened between us…" said Masterson. "Make up your mind: either you're a lawman, or you aren't. Don't make me look bad in front of Kreeger."

"I'll go," said Applejack, "but I won't like it."

"Say, what is this…" began Kreeger.

"My deputy gave his word," said Masterson. "That's enough for me. I'm giving the lad expense money, and suppose you get a packhorse and the supplies you need and go at it. I figure between the two of you, you'll get the job done."

That afternoon the two men rode out; Applejack leading a pack mule.

"We'll head for the pass," said Kreeger. "Peacock's been hitting travelers there. I figure he might have a hideout near one of the mining camps."

For three days they rode and stopped and spent the nights under the stars. Kreeger didn't manage but a few necessary words. Applejack kept his mouth shut, knowing which way the wind was blowing. Kreeger didn't trust or like him. Most of it was because of his age, surmised the younger lawman. If the hard case was going to test him, so be it. On the third evening of steady riding back and forth along the twenty-seven mile trail between Raton and Trinidad, with infrequent stops to rest or take sustenance, Kreeger finally spoke up.

"Alright, kid, so you're not a blatherer. I'll give you

that. We'll camp here for the night. Those rocks ought to hide our cook fire. You fix the grub; I'll make the coffee."

It was then that they heard gunfire, and it was close. They were on high ground above the trail.

"Leave the pack mule," whispered Kreeger. "You take the back trail and I'll take this side. Stay hidden, and if it's them, let me make the first move."

The upper ridge was pretty steep, and after separating, Applejack dismounted and led his horse. Coming down towards the main trail, he saw three men in masks holding up a group of freight wagons. The three holdup men were on foot and a fourth masked man, further off the trail, was mounted and holding reins of three horses. Tying off his mount, the lawman proceeded forward, keeping to cover.

Teamsters operating their bull trains were not easy men to stop. Most were hardened war veterans and sharpshooters. Somehow this gang of thieves got the drop on them. The head freighter was shouting at the robbers, and when one of the wagon drivers grabbed for a rifle, the lead outlaw turned and fanned his pistol, putting three pellets dead center in the freighter's chest.

"No more of that!" shouted the thief. "Now hand over your money belts! It's that or your life!"

Hearing the rough voice of the outlaw and seeing how he shot the freighter, Applejack was certain it was Bill Peacock, the man they were looking for.

Stepping closer, Applejack stopped and waited for Kreeger to make his move.

"This is the law!" shouted a voice from the rocks above. "You men are surrounded; drop your guns!"

The thieves had no intention of giving up. The man on the horse turned but could see no one to shoot at. Still, he made a snap shot into the brush. Kreeger, in hiding, fired his rifle, and the thief fell from his mount. The outlaws' horses reacted in unison and all four ran up the trail.

"You three!" shouted Kreeger still from cover. "Give it up!"

Two of the holdup men turned and fired toward the sound of the voice. Several teamsters, used to ambushes, grabbed their rifles and emptied their loads. The two robbers were dead before they hit the ground. The leader turned, stooped, and disappeared behind brush. He ran downhill. Applejack could hear him approaching. Bill Peacock's bandanna was torn off his face as he passed through a thicket of cedar. The outlaw ran towards Jack and the deputy stepped out.

"Hello, Bill," said Applejack.

Peacock slid to a stop. Dust kicked up around the older man and then a slight breeze dissipated the smoke-like cloud.

"I thought we'd meet one of these days," said Bill. "Is that a badge you're wearing, Jack?"

"It is."

"Unfortunate for you," said Bill, dropping a heavy money belt.

The young deputy and the outlaw stood facing each other. And then Bill broke the silence.

"You were always a quiet one, for a kid," said Bill. "I'm taking the money, Jack. You can try to stop me if you have to, but I'd prefer you just…"

"It's my job, Bill."

"Then make your move. I'm kind of in a hurry, and

I've got to find a horse."

"No, sir. I won't draw first."

In a blur of motion, Bill reached for his pistol and Applejack copied his move. The younger man was a split second faster getting his revolver up, and he fanned the hammer, the very pistol that Bill himself had filed for that purpose. The first bullet of Jack's hit dead center and three more struck close around it. Bill fanned one round into the ground and then fell backwards. The deputy ran to him and knelt down.

"Looks like you've been practicing," said Bill. There was a long escape of air and the older man was dead.

Applejack remained kneeling for some time, ignoring repeated calls from Kreeger. Getting to his feet, the deputy walked toward his partner. The other lawman was bleeding from a wound in his leg. Kreeger had wrapped a bandanna around it.

"Can you believe it?" said the deputy sheriff. "One of those shots hit me while I was hidden back in the brush."

Kreeger limped closer and looked down at Bill Peacock.

"I see that Masterson didn't exaggerate. If you don't mind, kid," said the older lawman, "I'll shake your hand now."

Applejack said nothing, just turned and started for his horse.

"Where you going, Jack?" shouted Kreeger. "You know there's a big reward on this man?"

Chapter 10

Early the next morning, Kreeger and Applejack rode into Trinidad, leading four horses. Bill Peacock and the three other outlaws were draped over their mounts. A crowd of people gathered and followed the cavalcade to the City Marshal's Office.

Not saying anything, Bat Masterson appeared and walked around the horses of the four dead men, observing their faces.

"Good job," said Masterson. "I just sent someone for a doctor. He should be here soon."

"Thanks," said Kreeger. "My leg's torn up pretty bad."

"Which one of you got Peacock?" asked Masterson.

Neither mounted lawman responded.

"It was you, wasn't it?" said the marshal, turning to his deputy.

"Sir, I had no choice."

"Be lucky, Jack, that it was Bill who taught you how to shoot, because I'm certain that not me or Kreeger or another deputy could have faced him down."

"I'm not feeling so lucky at the moment," replied Applejack.

"Well, you should," said Masterson. "There's a reward on him, and once we split it between us, you'll still have a good chunk. Not enough to get that ranch I've heard you talking about, but a start."

"Now wait a minute," said Kreeger. "I don't mind splitting the reward money with Jack, but not with you and the rest of your mob."

"Kreeger, the only reason you got Peacock is because of my man. Shut your mouth and take your share, or get nothing."

There was a long silence, and finally the deputy sheriff snarled: "All right, Masterson, I see your point. But mark my word, I'm going to take your job from you."

"Kreeger," replied Bat Masterson. "If this town wants you over me, then so be it!"

"Do I patrol tonight?" asked Applejack.

"It's your job, Jack. You'll partner with Flint again," said the marshal.

A doctor came running with his black bag.

"It's about time," said Kreeger, dismounting and showing the doc his wounded leg.

Applejack left his pack mule with a deputy and rode up the street and toward his shack. He would steel himself for the night shift. The further he rode away from the commotion, the quieter it became.

That night, nothing much was said as the two deputies patrolled the town and checked doors. Applejack didn't volunteer and Flint didn't push him about what happened up on Raton Pass.

After his duty ended for the night, Applejack went back to his little cabin. Physically and mentally exhausted, he lay down. For many hours he slept, and then, during the height of a bad dream, he sat upright, wide awake. In his nightmare he had relived the shooting that took place between Bill 'Smith' Peacock and himself. Wiping sweat from his face, Jack arose and poured himself a drink of water. Unable to sleep, he began to pace. Walking back and forth and then in a circle in the close confines of the little cabin, he attempted to subdue his nervous energy.

Star and moonlight illuminated his quarters through a narrow window. One of those winds that so often blow around southern Colorado began to pick up. The thirty-mile gusts rattled and whined, and it fit his mood. In the twilight, Jack came to a halt, stopped, and thought about what he had done and what it meant to be a law officer. The way he felt at the moment, he would gladly lay aside his badge and go back to his parent's hardscrabble ranch. He would do anything that didn't involve having to face down or kill another person. But he knew, at the moment, that he had an obligation to Bat Masterson for as long as he remained the elected marshal. After all, Masterson had given him a job when he needed it most; and besides, he needed the money to start another ranch.

A sudden feeling of exhaustion supplanted the burst of nervous energy, and Applejack collapsed back down on his bed. There he lay and thought; and after a long interval, fell asleep.

Chapter 11

"The reward for Peacock works out to $800 apiece," explained Masterson to the deputies standing in his office. "You've got Jack to thank for that money and, far as I see it, for saving us all from one bad gunman."

Applejack reluctantly took the envelope of money and, unlike the rest, marched directly to the bank to deposit every penny. He had liked Bill, and the young deputy couldn't help thinking that it was a terrible waste. Walking back to his horse, he mounted and rode alone towards the target range up on Raton Pass. When he arrived, the other deputies were already there. He immediately noticed a different attitude in the men. Flint came over and explained why.

"It's one thing to show some fancy target shooting," said Flint, "but another to face a man down. The fellers been talking, we figure you're one of us now. And besides, we're all grateful for the money."

That morning, Applejack was in a bad mood, and when it was his turn to shoot, the lead bullets drifted from the target and did not hit their mark. The others, including the marshal, looked on, then Masterson reacted.

"Jack! Doesn't matter how you feel; you're a lawman and you've got a job to do. Our lives depend on how you shoot. Now snap out of it, reload, and hit your target, or quit."

In evident anger, Jack reloaded his revolver, stepped

up to the firing line, and as quick as a few heart beats, fanned his pistol. Each bullet hit dead center.

"That's better," said Masterson.

The young deputy mounted his horse and rode down the mountain. The other lawmen watched him go.

"Looks like his heart's not in it," said Flint.

"Give him time," said Masterson. "Each of us handles a shooting in our own way."

Chapter 12

Applejack didn't know it, but his face had changed. Youth and innocence disappeared and was replaced with new lines and a hard cast. When he walked his shift with Flint, he no longer had a cavalier attitude. Gone was the casual saunter along the street. Now each echoing noise or movement sent him to peak vigilance, and his heart fluttered. It stopped only when he'd confirmed there was no danger. Being a deputy marshal was taking a toll on the young man. Although he had thought about these many issues separately, he now put them together into a compilation of factors.

Trinidad was in the land of the Utes, and remnants of one large tribe refused to go to the reservation. Often they came into town to hang around and observe. And outside the city boundary, with good cause, some Indians harassed travelers for food and other items. The town was also near the large Spanish land grants, and there were the rich Bacas and their workers who traveled from New Mexico into the city for entertainment. For years, outlaws had used the town as a place of amusement. With the coming of the big coal companies and the foreign workers, Trinidad took on a new flavor and increasing wealth. Raton Pass continued to attract wagon trains. The arrival of the railroad in the late 70s, brought droves of pioneers and businessmen moving west.

Realizing these many issues for the first time, Applejack started the next night's shift with greater apprehension.

"Hey, Jack," called Flint when they began their rounds. "I've never known you to be so jumpy."

"Working with Kreeger was bad enough," said Applejack, "but meeting up with…

"Peacock?" said Flint.

"Yeah. It affects a man, doesn't it?"

"You had good cause," said Flint. "It was you or him."

"I know that, but it doesn't make it any easier."

"Killing your first man changes everything," said Flint, speaking in a softer tone. "You proved yourself."

"Nothing I'm proud of."

"No, but it makes you one of us, now. It takes courage to face down a man shooting back at you."

"It would have been better if I hadn't known him," said Applejack.

"If you'd let your guard down and talk to us now and then, you'd learn that nearly each one of us had to go after someone we knew. It comes with the job."

Applejack looked away.

"Thanks, Flint. But I got all these new thoughts running through my head. And they won't stop. I appreciate what you're saying, but the job doesn't seem so easy anymore."

"Jack," said the older deputy. "You got to ease up or you're going to wear yourself out. Stop being so jumpy and quit second-guessing yourself. Trust your instincts. Besides, there's two of us to face what comes up."

Through the rest of the night, Flint and Jack made their rounds. And with this new level of maturity, Applejack continued to think about the situation he was in knowing that each day they put their lives on the line, it was hard to imagine the townspeople turning against them.

The citizens of Trinidad began to look on the officers as an unnecessary liability, and wanted them gone. The press and voters complained of the lawmen's gambling, excessive drinking, and hard behavior. They were the exact type of gunmen needed to change a lawless community; but not the kind wanted once it was tamed. It was evident it would not be long before they would all lose their jobs.

Applejack felt like a traitor. Now that he was accepted as being one of them, he wished that he wasn't. He couldn't wait to be riding the range and to have the simple task of herding stock or performing daily ranch work. When Bat Masterson was elected out of office, the young man would positively quit the law for keeps.

Chapter 13

The Sunday afternoon meetings with the priest were becoming more interesting. The shyness and the uncomfortable feeling Applejack once had in Father Munnecom's presence disappeared. Over time, the young man became less reticent and more animated over the discussion of books the religious man had given him to read. Occasionally both would forget about time, and they would talk late into the evening. And it was the wise choice of beginning with *The Count of Monte Cristo* that gave the unworldly young man his start.

On the other side of the coin was the priest's motivation. He was pleased with Jack's growing academic knowledge; but more than that, with his growing maturity about human behavior. Complicit in young Jack's education was the priest's own desires to confront Alfonso Martinez in his own way, and that was through the innocent Maria and the young deputy.

Father Munnecom was well aware of his human foibles and his mismatch with a mostly Spanish-speaking community. From the very beginning, he voiced his objections to his superiors. The orders stood, and the priest assigned to the Trinidad church wondered just how long he would last.

People talked and rumors spread. And his nefarious business deals and investments about town caused a growing resistance from certain parishioners, especially Alfonso Martinez. Applejack increasingly became the priest's one most pleasant and welcome distraction. Teaching and helping the young man to court a Spanish land grant daughter, especially when it infuriated Martinez, pleased the clergyman's Machiavellian side. Not everything is as it seems.

On one Sunday afternoon, the good Father broached the subject of Maria Martinez and her family. It quickly became a heated conversation.

"Father," said Applejack. "It's hopeless, isn't it? I have nothing to offer, and I am not of the right station to gain the respect and consent of her father."

"Well said, Jack," replied the priest. "Knowing that, what do you propose to do?"

"I'm saving money. I have nine hundred dollars, but I know it is not enough to purchase the type of ranch I want."

"One with water?"

"Yes."

"In other words," said the priest, "A ranch large enough to make you a man of means?"

"Yes, that too, Father; but only because of Maria."

"Then perhaps together we can find a way to make that happen," said Father Munnecom.

"What you have been teaching me is more than enough. No one has been as helpful as you."

"Come, it's late. Next time we can discuss more about this. For right now, here's another book to read. It's by Mark Twain and it's called *Roughing It*. It has quite a bit of humor, and I find it enlightening. Something I am sure you will enjoy. I can't wait until our next meeting to review it."

"Thank you, Father," said Applejack, and together

priest and deputy went to the door.

The young lawman walked down the street to his shack and got ready for his rounds. An hour later, he met Flint at the marshal's office, and together they began their patrol. That night he tried to push away the constant thoughts of the killing. Instead, he struggled to focus on the woman he sought. Knowing full well the impossibility of it, Jack did what he had done since first seeing Maria. He projected himself into a future when he could actually be able to meet and be with her.

Foolish or not, thought Jack. *That's the way it is. I've got to quit this job before it continues to change me.*

Chapter 14

As it is with all young people who are presented with obstacles, Applejack began to search for a way to communicate with the girl of his affections. A week later, by accident, he observed Maria Martinez riding a spirited black gelding. With her were two armed male chaperons. A sudden burst of inspiration came to the young man, and from a hill, he could see the direction the three riders were headed. Galloping his stallion across the prairie, he came upon the very trail they were riding. When they approached, Applejack slowed his mount, removed his hat, and spoke to the riders.

"Gentlemen, dear lady," declared Applejack, and then he smiled and returned his hat to his head.

The young deputy rode past them, his gaze focused on Maria. He watched as she raised her veil for him to see her smile. Jack went home and composed a message. The next time he saw her was on a Thursday. She was riding ahead of her guards, and Applejack was able to pass her a note.

The first message was one including a poem by Elizabeth Barrett Browning. It came from a book provided by Father Munnecom. Jack would tell no living person of this exchange; not even the good priest. The words he gave her were nearly memorized.

My Dear Maria,

Forgive me for this courtship from afar, but as you

know, I am forbidden to approach without permission. I tried, and through no fault of my own, it went very badly. Please let me say that from the very first moment I saw you, I was greatly affected, and with each passing moment my fondness has grown stronger until there is hardly anything else I can think of. If I may be so bold, Elizabeth Browning relates my feelings so much better than I ever could.
Your humble servant,
Applejack Martin

How do I love thee? Let me count the ways.
I love thee to the depth and breadth and height
My soul can reach, when feeling out of sight
For the ends of Being and ideal Grace.
I love thee to the level of every day's
Most quiet need, by sun and candlelight.
I love thee freely, as men strive for Right;
I love thee purely, as they turn from Praise.
I love with a passion put to use
In my old griefs, and with my childhood's faith.
I love thee with a love I seemed to lose
With my lost saints, I love thee with the breath,
Smiles, tears, of all my life! And, if God choose,
I shall but love thee better after death.

(Please, when you can, leave a response in the opening of the tall rock near where I passed this note to you).

The next day and for many days afterwards, Jack went to the rock and found the opening devoid of any message. More than a week passed, and there was still no response.

Crestfallen, Applejack's morose emotions consumed him. She didn't care to respond. Obviously, she had no real feelings for him.

He thought of quitting his job, taking his money, and riding far from this land. Maybe Oregon was a place to make a new start, or even Canada. That night he patrolled the town, and after work he considered buying a bottle and joining his fellow deputies in drink. Although less conspicuous about it, there was one saloon where the lawmen always hung out in the back room, gambling, drinking, and occasionally consorting with lady friends. After his duty, Jack did go to the saloon, but could not bring himself to enter. Instead, he walked past the establishment, out of town, and onto the prairie.

It was that special moment when a pre-dawn light began to brighten the horizon, but the heavens remained dark and stars continued to shine and flicker down upon those wise enough to take the time to look. Jack walked slowly and aimlessly out into the dry desert landscape. His emotions overwhelmed him; his thoughts a jumble of confusion. He did not know it, but he was like every young man who ever had to decide what direction his footsteps would take him. Literally, what he chose to do at this moment would decide the future of his entire life. Should he run away? Or should he stay? Did anybody really care, or was it all up to him?

The sky began to lighten. From far off a lone wolf howled a long, mournful cry. In answer came the high piercing yips from a pack of coyotes. A shadow glided over the young man and he looked up. It was an owl with wide-sweeping wings that disappeared into the cedars. The owl must have landed, for it began to hoot forlornly.

An involuntary shiver passed over Jack. Nature was waiting for dark to turn to daylight, and the land and animal sounds he was so familiar with fit his mood and troubled thoughts.

The hard adobe ground crunched under his feet, and as the sun rose from the east, the air began to warm. Not heeding his movement, needing to release his emotions, he walked and walked, and it wasn't until he brushed against a large jumping cholla that he became aware of his surroundings. A piece broke off and its sharp thorns embedded itself through his canvass pants and into his right thigh. The pain was intense and Jack stopped. Foolishly putting fingers to the piece of cactus, he yelped and let go.

"Why you..." exclaimed Jack, "you dumb idiot!"

Pulling spines carefully from his fingers, he watched the blood ooze from tiny holes. And then, taking his pistol, he placed the barrel underneath one loose end of the cactus and gently pried. Working at it, he deftly managed to remove the entire thorny piece, and it fell to the ground. Holstering the pistol, Applejack carefully began pulling pieces of spine that remained stuck through his pants and into his thigh. When done, he sighed and then, still in pain, found a large rock and sat down.

"What are you doing, you fool?" asked the young man out loud to himself.

Arising from the boulder and looking around, Applejack tried to identify in which direction lay Trinidad and his cabin. Then, limping slightly, he headed back. This time, aware of his surroundings, he avoided the small prickly pear clumps that lay close to the ground and the large bunches of jumping cholla cactus.

Once back at the shack, he found water and some dried jerky. He ate and drank. Going to the private barn behind his cabin, he saddled Bucky and rode in the direction of where Maria took her daily rides. After a time, Applejack came to the rock. In the hole he found a beige parchment that was not his. Astride his horse, he broke a red seal of candle wax. His hands shook as he nervously began to read. For a moment, his vision blurred.

My Dear Señor Jack,
Unlike your people, it is not often that we express affection so publicly and so quickly. But I did notice you as you noticed me. And, as time has gone by, I could not help but see your continued attention towards myself. It has been many months now, and although we come from two distinct cultures, I too, am attracted. If only there was a way... Thank you for the beautiful poem, I keep your message close and read it often.
Until our next exchange.
Maria

All thought of leaving immediately disappeared. Holding the message tightly in his hands, he stared at it for some time and then carefully buttoned it in his shirt and next to his heart. Mounting Bucky, he rode into the brush and, a short while later, watched as Maria Martinez and her two guards rode past. As he guided his horse along, a smile crossed his face for the first time in a long while. He was indeed a very changed man.

Chapter 15

Applejack's mood and personality seemed to have altered. For a young man who seldom spoke or smiled, there was a complete transformation. Bat Masterson and his deputies were amazed at the happy disposition Jack displayed. Father Munnecom also could not help but notice the sudden change. He attributed it to some secret exchange between his young friend and Maria Martinez.

"Come, Jack," questioned the priest. "What happened since we last spoke?"

"I can't say, Father, and I won't."

"Applejack!" exclaimed the clergyman. "I am absolutely astonished. I thought that you and I had developed a trusting friendship."

"There are some things a man cannot divulge, even to his closest friend. Perhaps one day I will, but not now."

"Can't you at least give me a hint?"

"No, Father. What is that word? It would not be chivalrous."

"Ahh, just as I suspected: it has something to do with a certain lady."

"Let's change the subject, Father. You gave me a book to read. Suppose we discuss that."

"If you insist, but not before telling you that if you are breaking the decorum of proper behavior with young Maria Martinez, your path to courting her may be severely compromised."

"I'll keep that in mind," replied Applejack.

All through the afternoon Father Munnecom and his student discussed the life of Mark Twain and analyzed the book *Roughing It.* Applejack was slowly realizing what it would take to become a literate man. He questioned at what point he might ever become a suitable prospect for Maria.

The days and weeks slipped by. Without fail, Applejack attended church, and every glimpse of Maria drove him to further effort. The notes were progressing, and although they were very few, the young suitor was encouraged. With the hopeful promise that someday Maria might be by his side, Applejack felt there was nothing he could not accomplish.

Because he worked nights, he was able to espy her riding habits, and although she did not ride every day, he was sure to get a glimpse of her on Mondays, Wednesdays, and Thursdays. It was on a Thursday, while the young deputy was observing her approach with the two guards, that the assault began.

From his hiding place, Applejack could look down over the trail. He saw the approach of Maria; and behind her were the two vaqueros. Both had rifles in scabbards, pistols, and one always wore a full bandolier. As the young deputy watched, one guard suddenly slumped and fell off his horse. The sound of a rifle echoed across the land. This was followed by repeated shots. The second guard twisted violently and fell. Both horses, now frightened, galloped away and disappeared over a slope.

Maria turned and looked to the fallen vaqueros. She sat, hand to her mouth in horror. Then, realizing her situation, she slapped reins and dug spurs into the mount's side. Four men appeared from behind, riding at full gallop. They quickly overcame the young woman, grabbed the bridle, and forced horse and rider to a stop.

Applejack acted without thought. Running to Bucky, he pulled a Winchester from its scabbard, and from his position, he aimed carefully, fired, and one abductor fell. Jack levered another round and shot a second rider. The two remaining men, still holding the halter on both sides of the girl's mount, were too close to her for the young man to shoot safely. Jack placed the rifle back in the scabbard, untied reins, and mounted. He raced his horse towards the outlaws and skidded to a halt not more than fifteen feet from the men and the young woman. The deputy jumped down and slapped Bucky away. His marshal's badge clearly showed under the bright light of the sun and one of the kidnappers yelled out.

"Señor, that badge has no power here."

"Release Maria and I'll let you live," replied Applejack.

Both banditos laughed.

"Big talk for such a young gringo," said the kidnapper, looking down.

"You killed my compadres," exclaimed the other, "and now I kill you!"

Both outlaws let go of Maria's horse and began to draw their revolvers. Applejack stood, feet apart, his right hand near his pistol. He drew and fanned two quick shots at the outlaw to his right and then two more at the gunman on his left. Hit dead center, the men were driven from their saddles and, as before, the frightened horses screamed and fled.

"Quickly, Señor Applejack," said Maria. "We must see to my companions."

Jack called to Bucky, and the horse came running towards him. They rode back to the fallen guards. The deputy dismounted and checked on one, then the other.

"I am afraid," he said, "they are both dead."

"¡Dios mío!" exclaimed Maria.

"Did you know those outlaws?" asked Jack, reloading his pistol.

"Sí," replied Maria. "I knew the big one. His name was Pedro and he once worked for my father. He was fired for not doing his job."

"I suppose they were kidnapping you for ransom?" asked Applejack.

"Sí, my father...he is...very rich. He owns ranches and much land here and in New Mexico. He was afraid of something like this and didn't want me riding. When I insisted, he ordered Francisco and Antonio to guard me."

"It was a good thing I was watching or..."

"You saved my life, Jack. For that, I am very grateful."

"It was providence. Your guards' horses have run away, and I am afraid I cannot bring your men back to your house. But I am sure your father will see to that. Come, I will take you home."

Maria, despite the shootings and the grief over her comrades, momentarily raised her veil and smiled at her rescuer.

"Señor, I see why the famous lawman has hired one so young. You are very brave and so good with your pistolas."

"I am afraid it was all a matter of luck."

"Then, señor," replied Maria, "I am also thankful for such luck."

Maria turned her horse in the direction of her father's

hacienda and Applejack followed. He took in the full picture of this lovely girl and did it shyly, but with great admiration. She rode sidesaddle on a handsome black thoroughbred that stepped lively and daintily on its spindly legs. The young woman wore a black dress that fell across the withers and belly of the horse. On her head was a black hat that did not completely hide her sleek raven hair, done up neatly under it. She held a closed umbrella in one hand and the reins in the other. Occasionally, she tapped the hind quarters of her mount with the umbrella's tip, urging the animal into a trot. She rode well, despite her precarious position on the strange saddle. The flowing dress could not hide her ample figure—or the dark veil conceal her lovely features.

For a long time neither spoke, and when the silence became almost unbearable for the young man, he rode up next to her and searched in vain for something to say.

"You must speak to me, señor; it may be our only chance for a long while, or perhaps forever. My father is a very strict man. He follows tradition and is extremely proud. Perhaps…too proud. I don't think after this he will allow me to go riding."

"No doubt," replied the young man, not knowing what else to say.

"Oh, Jack, how I have hungered for every glimpse of you at church."

"It is exactly the same with me, Maria. I don't know how I will break down the barriers with your father. I love you with all my heart. You have shown your lovely face before, so why now do you hide behind that veil? Please, let me at least see your face again and touch your hand."

Maria stopped her horse. Momentarily it pranced on four legs in nervous energy, and then stood stiffly. She held reins firmly with her left hand, and with her right, holding the umbrella, she raised her veil. Turning her head so Jack could see, she watched him as he moved Bucky closer. He took her gloved hand and held it around the handle of the umbrella, an impediment he ignored. He looked down into her face, and she looked up into his.

"It is greatly forbidden that I ride with my face uncovered. Father is very strict and thinks he is protecting me. I know he will ask, and I have been taught never to lie. But in this, in this one thing, if he asks, I will not speak. Applejack is such a funny little name. Perhaps one day you will explain. Jack, I give you permission to kiss me."

"Are you sure, Maria?"

"Oh yes! Hurry! Kiss me!"

Applejack did as she asked. He leaned forward from his horse and bent down and touched his lips to hers. Letting go of reins, still holding her right hand, he put his left around her body and pulled her to him. He kissed her with all the strength and vigor he had in him. Letting go when her horse began to move, she found her seat and sat upright.

"Oh Jack!" Maria exclaimed. "You take my breath! If nothing else, for the rest of my life, I shall remember your kiss and embrace."

He smiled and watched in disappointment as she lowered her veil. They resumed their journey, this time at a fast walk.

"Jack, you must promise not to ever..."

"I promise, Maria. I shall never tell a living soul that

we touched, and God will be our sole witness."

"Yes, only him," said Maria.

"I have not even told Father Munnecom about the notes."

"You are a friend of the good Father? You speak to him?"

"Yes, every Sunday at four we meet. He gives me books and then we discuss them at length. He has taught me a great deal..."

"This is all so very strange and wonderful. Has he explained why?"

"Yes. He told me I was in need of a friend, and that he would make a good one. Several times he has offered to help me find a way to court you."

"Oh!" said Maria. "This gives me great hope. With the priest on our side, perhaps there will be a way. I have prayed over this matter so many times."

"I've been wondering," said Jack. "What does your mother think about the two of us? Would she be willing to intervene and persuade your father?"

"Oh, no!" exclaimed Maria. "Ma-ma would never go against Father's wishes in any matters."

The horses snorted as riders approached. It was Maria's father, and behind him were two armed vaqueros. The arriving horses skidded to a halt as reins were pulled violently. From the expression on Señor Martinez's face, Applejack knew he was in trouble.

"So! This is how you betray me?" shouted the father. "How much did you pay Antonio and Francisco? I shall lash them until they can no longer stand! I'll make them walk away on foot in humiliation! How dare you meet this gunman! Shame on you, Maria! Against all that Ma-

ma and…"

"Father! Please! You don't understand!"

"You dare to shout at me! To interrupt your own father? Go, Maria, from my sight before I do something…"

"Oh, Father!"

"Go!" screamed the incensed parent.

Hesitantly, Maria looked to the young man, then her father, and, bowing her head, she turned her horse and rode away.

"Señor Martinez!" exclaimed Applejack. "You have it wrong. Maria was…"

"How dare you say my daughter's first name in my presence! You…you…scoundrel!"

Martinez leaned forward and with a leather horse crop, repeatedly and violently struck at Applejack. The first strike hit him squarely across the left cheek and it instantly cut and drew blood. Lifting hand and arm in protection, Jack received more blows, raising welts and drawing even more blood.

Applejack backed Bucky away from the attack and began to shout.

"You hotheaded fool!" yelled Jack. "Your daughter faced a kidnapping! Antonio and Francisco were killed!

"If that is so," shouted the father. "How did you…"

"I happened along and stopped them."

"I bet you were spying!"

"Doesn't matter, there were four of them and…"

"And I suppose you are going to tell me you killed them all."

"I did."

"I don't…believe…how could one of your age…"

"Ask your daughter, she'll tell you."

"I will! Carlos, Juan! Go with this scoundrel and see if he is telling the truth. If he is, bring home the bodies. I am going back to speak to Maria."

Applejack led the vaqueros to where the two guards lay. He also showed them the four dead outlaws. They recognized Pedro's body. Both Carlos and Juan swore in Spanish. Leaving them to figure out how to retrieve the two dead guards, Jack pushed his horse hard. He galloped into Trinidad and up to the marshal's office.

"Well?" asked Bat Masterson. "Judging by your face and all that blood, I'd say you've been through it. Since there's an ordinance against racing a horse through town, what do you have to say for yourself?"

Applejack told Masterson the entire story and then gave exact directions as to where the outlaw's bodies lay.

"You've had quite a day of it, Applejack," said the marshal. "But just how did you happen to be near that young lady in the first place? Never mind. I'll be speaking to Martinez. Suppose you go and rest; you have patrol in a few hours, and I bet you've had no sleep at all."

"Sir," said Applejack. "I'd prefer if you not talk to Maria's father."

"Jack," replied Masterson. "You're my deputy and I don't let any man disrespect the badge or the law, no matter who they are."

Chapter 16

That evening while Applejack policed the business district of town, checking doors, he did it in a great deal of pain. His face, arms, and hands burned like fire, and it was becoming worse. The places where the crop struck were swollen and red. Flint, who walked with Jack, noticed his discomfort. The older deputy came nearer and offered advice.

"Kid, after this go-around, we better stop at the office and put balm on those wounds. I bet they hurt something fierce."

"Yes, they do."

"I'm afraid that cut on your face is getting nasty. What were you hit with?"

"A riding crop."

"And you didn't shoot the…"

"He was the father, and I couldn't…"

Flint laughed out loud.

"I get it. That's how some fathers act, even if you did save his daughter's life. He really struck you good. That cut on your face is going to leave a scar for sure."

The two deputies walked their rounds and came up to the marshal's office. Inside, Flint pulled a fairly clean rag and a bottle of whiskey from a desk drawer.

"This is Masterson's. I hope he won't mind," said Flint.

The deputy pulled the cork, wet the rag with whiskey, and motioned Jack to sit at the desk.

"Now, hold still, this may burn a bit."

Flint pressed firmly, and Applejack jerked back. The older deputy laughed again.

"Hold still—you don't want this to get infected any worse than it already is. One more time, for affect."

Again Flint wet the rag and applied it firmly to the cheek and pressed. All the while he held Jack by one arm. Again the young deputy flinched. Ignoring his partner's complaints, the older lawman wet the rag repeatedly and began applying it to cuts on Jack's hands, and to several deep lacerations on his arms.

"You should have done this right after you were struck," said Flint. "It looks like every one of them is becoming infected. In the morning you better go see the doc."

"I don't like doctors," replied Applejack.

"Maybe not, but he'll have something better than this whiskey. We've got some Sloan's Liniment, if you want to try that."

"No, the whiskey burns enough. Although it is letting up a bit."

"The alcohol will stop some of the infection. Do as I say; see the doc tomorrow."

Flint put the whiskey away and took the rag outside and threw it in the trash. Together the lawmen continued their rounds, and in the morning they were relieved of duty. Applejack, still suffering from the pain of his infected wounds, went and saw a doctor. The medical man cleaned them with stinging alcohol, repeating what Flint had said about the need to have received earlier treatment. The doc also mentioned that when healed, he would have a prominent scar across his face. Jack was given a jar of soothing balm, and the doctor applied some of it before the deputy returned to his shack and bed.

It was a restless sleep, and through visions of flames, armed men with pistols walked out of a burning inferno to shoot at the young lawman. Applejack did his best to fire back at the many figures with blazing guns. Repeatedly, the young man awoke and wiped sweat from his fevered face, and several times sought water to drink. He lay back down and slept in fitful bouts only to awaken drenched and in pain from his many infected wounds. Finally he gave up trying to sleep, and at noon applied some of the soothing balm. He returned to bed, stared at the crude wooden ceiling, and thought about Maria.

Applejack wondered what she was thinking. Was she also troubled with nightmares? Was she regretting the conversation and the kiss he had given her? In the light of day, was she rethinking her affection for a man who could so easily take the lives of four men? Even if they were killers and brutes who tried to kidnap her? And, what about her father? Would she do as he demanded, and try to forget any thought of a relationship?

Chapter 17

Jack didn't know it, but at that very moment Marshal Bat Masterson walked from his office up the street to the Catholic Church. Knocking on the door of the rectory, the marshal was met by the housekeeper. She listened for a moment and then went in search of the priest. Father Munnecom came to the door and, surprised by the visit, invited the lawman to his office.

"Have you heard?" asked Masterson.

"It is a small town, marshal," replied the priest.

"That young man is the best deputy I have ever had. I am going to miss him when I leave."

"I am pleased you are not taking him with you. Are you aware that he plans to quit the law profession?"

"I am not completely dense, Father. I know he wants a ranch. And I am guessing he thinks it is the one avenue that will enable him to court that Martinez gal he has been moping about. And I also know that since his first killing, he has been very troubled. It was only his affection for that gal that has...shall we say...redeemed him."

"Quite an astute assessment, marshal. I find Jack to be a very moral and intelligent young man. It is astonishing he has this ability with weapons. However, how remarkable and fortunate that he was able to defend and save the girl."

"I don't think these killings will have the effect the first one had," replied Masterson. "Were you aware he knew Bill Peacock?"

"Yes. There isn't much I don't know about young Jack Martin. You may not realize it, but I have gained his confidence and trust. Not an easy thing to do. We have been meeting on Sundays and I tutor him in literature and other subjects. He learns quickly."

"I was aware, and I wondered what it was about. Perhaps, if you are willing, we can both find a way to help this kid. But first, I need your assistance with Martinez. Even though Applejack saved his daughter, he had the effrontery to beat Jack. I can't let that go. No man assaults one of my law officers."

"Yes, I heard this, and I have been thinking that we can turn this to young Jack's advantage. Especially in the courtship of Martinez's daughter."

"Interesting. I was going to ask you to go with me and help me talk to this arrogant varmint. And, if I may, Father Munnecom, reliable informants have come to me to tell of a priest who likes to gamble and to make investments."

"Really? Do you believe everything you hear?"

"When the informants are reliable. And, if true, I do believe I can make certain arrangements that will benefit us both. I have many contacts in this town."

"Marshal Masterson," said the Father, breaking into a broad smile, "although I am a priest, I do not want to retire a pauper when I return to Europe. I have some gambling enterprises, monies to invest, and land to divest, and I would appreciate any help in this matter. I've been looking for a discreet person I could trust to assist me."

"Excellent," replied the marshal. "I am sure I can. If

we're to continue, you wouldn't by any chance have strong spirits hiding in that desk of yours?"

"I do, I do," said Father Munnecom, taking out a key and opening a wide lower drawer. He withdrew a whiskey bottle and two glasses.

"So, you have heard talk of my other activities?"

"I have," replied Masterson, cautiously.

"Let me explain," said Munnecom. "I didn't expect to be sent all the way from Holland, to this...shall we say...Wild West. My proclivities are that of a cultured man. I like my books, to be surrounded by men of great reason, and to have challenging discussions. And, of course, I like my creature comforts. To put it more bluntly: before I die, I would like to travel greater Europe, visit museums and art galleries, and converse with great writers and men of learning. It takes a man of means to accomplish such goals."

"You don't have to explain to me, Father," said Masterson.

"Oh, but I do. It is better that you understand my motivations."

"Perhaps you're right," replied the marshal.

"I don't believe in happenstance. I think it fortuitous that we meet now, and at this exact moment."

"If you say so, Father," replied Masterson. "I never turn down a good business deal when the opportunity presents itself."

"Pleased to hear it," said the man of cloth. "Now, as to Applejack, I think between the two of us, we can find a solution and a better future for our young friend. Do you mind if I close the door? Sometimes my housekeeper becomes a bit too curious."

The meeting between the priest and the marshal lasted a long time, and only they and a higher power knew what transpired. At the end of the meeting, the two men shook hands. Smiling, Marshal Masterson left the priest's residence, walked to the stables, and rented a buggy. He returned to pick up Father Munnecom, who was waiting. Masterson, reins in hand, watched as the priest climbed aboard. The Father sat back in comfort as the lawman guided the one-horse rig towards the hacienda of Alfonso Martinez.

Chapter 18

The deputies and Masterson met at the box canyon up on Raton Pass for another shooting session. While the other lawmen acted tough, drank to excess, and chased women, they had done nothing to match the actions and skill of the less worldly Applejack Martin. And when Jack arrived to join the group, the rough lawmen, along with Masterson, remained silent. This last episode of saving a girl from four killers was a feat worthy of respect. So the men watched in awe as Applejack loaded an extra round into his pistol and commenced firing at chalked silhouettes carved onto the rock wall. There were three characters drawn on the stone by one of the more irreverent lawmen; perhaps in crude jest. But Jack took no umbrage and, as fast as any gunmen alive, the deputy drew and fanned his pistol. Two bullets hit dead center in each of the three carvings. Calmly reloading his revolver, Jack looked around. The other lawmen remained reticent.

Then Flint came forward and thumped Applejack on the back.

"Here he is, fellows!" announced Flint. "Applejack Martin, lawman extraordinaire! Sure glad he's on our side!"

The deputies congratulated Jack, shaking his hand and talking all at once, and this included Masterson. Applejack was a bit overwhelmed, and the wounds on his hands, arms, and face still hurt. The handshaking did little to ease the pain. Jack watched as the men began target practice, shooting at the many empty liquor and store bottles. When they finished, they rode as a group down the mountain and into town. Jack was now indeed a trusted and respected member of Masterson's crew.

Riding to his shack, Applejack went inside, took a long drink of water, and laid down to sleep. For the first time since the attempted kidnapping, the deputy slept without dreaming. In the late afternoon, he awoke well rested. Washing up and changing clothes, Jack walked to the Alpine restaurant where he usually met Flint for their afternoon breakfast before policing the town.

Starting their duty and passing by a gun shop, Applejack nearly ran face to face into Maria's father, Alfonso Martinez. As usual, the man was colorfully dressed in Spanish garb, and he was holding the very crop with which he had struck the deputy. The arrogant expression Martinez wore was replaced with surprise as he stared at a spot on the deputy's face—the livid, unhealed wound. Applejack stood his ground and waited for the elder man to speak.

"You!" uttered the Spanish rancher. "Of all the peeples in this town, it had to be you! Soon, señor, I will personally deal with you."

Martinez, in anger, slapped his crop against his right leg. With his two guards, he marched to his splendidly adorned thoroughbred. The three mounted their horses and rode away.

"What was that about?" asked Flint, who was now standing next to Applejack. "It's a wonder you didn't knock that silly smirk off the man's face. After all, you owe him that."

"If it hadn't been for Maria…I might have …"

"Well, hoss, you've got more give then me. Why, I'd..."

"Never mind," exclaimed Jack. "Let's get back to work."

All through the week, Applejack and Flint performed their duty. Teaming up with the other deputies on Friday and Saturday night, they each had their hands full dealing with drunken cowboys and vaqueros who had brought in herds and ended up in Trinidad. As they looked for entertainment, fights would break out among the various drinking factions. It wasn't just Applejack, but Flint and the other deputies grew weary of the conflicts.

When the week was finished, Applejack was anxious to meet with Father Munnecom and tell him about the strange encounter with Martinez. The book they were to discuss was a new one by Mark Twain, *The Prince and the Pauper*. After Applejack arrived for his Sunday visit, he felt that the Father was acting a bit strange. Perhaps it was the fact that outside of being a deputy, Jack had saved Maria by killing four more men. Whatever it was, the deputy did not like the unusual speculative look and the annoying reflexive smile that appeared upon the priest's lips.

They talked about the attempted kidnapping and shooting. Father Munnecom kept asking what had transpired during the brief time Applejack was alone with Maria. The deputy said little, and went on to discuss the unfortunate altercation between himself and the arrogant father. The priest observed the wound on the young man's face and he also commented that it would leave a noticeable scar.

Their session extended into the evening, and not once

did they discuss Mark Twain's book. It was the priest who kept focusing on the subject of Maria.

"Applejack, you didn't tell me you told Maria we were friends and were meeting these many Sundays."

"No, and perhaps I shouldn't have told her," said Jack. "It just slipped. But she seemed excited when she found out. What did she say to you?"

"She asked if it was true; if I was planning to help you."

"And?"

"I told her I have already made my first attempt."

"What? But I don't understand."

"You will. You see, the marshal and I have spoken and come to some understanding on your behalf. Perhaps you don't know it, but like myself, he respects and likes you."

"I'm glad to hear it," said the young man. "And?"

"And...together we went to speak with Señor Martinez. I don't think we have all the details figured out, but since most of this was Masterson's idea, I thought it fitting that he explain what he has in mind for you."

"You what? I still don't understand," exclaimed Applejack. "What does Masterson have to do with any of this? This is confusing. What about Maria? What did she..."

"As to Marshal Masterson's interest in this, his first motive was to make it clear to Martinez that he would not have his deputies abused. As for Maria, I will tell you nothing at this point. What she told me was in strict confidence. As for speaking to her father, it took some doing, but I convinced (or should I say, the marshal and I convinced) the stubborn old man to at least listen to us."

"Yes? And?"

"Let me just say that it didn't go as well as expected."

This time there was a longer silence, and Applejack did nothing to break it. Finally Father Munnecom sighed and, standing up, he paced before a fireplace. It was January, and getting cooler. Flames crackled in the open hearth. The good Father placed his hands before the fire and rubbed them, and Jack stared at the priest's back.

"Señor Martinez made it clear that he thought you were nothing but a rash and uncouth gunman. I tried my best to explain that if it wasn't for your courageous interference, he would have no daughter. I went on to further explain that his rash behavior, given the circumstances, was totally inexcusable. Worse, that he had made a mark upon your face; a scar that you will bear forever. I told him, with some heat, that it was evidence of a grave injustice committed by the very man who should be the most grateful for having his daughter saved."

More silence.

"And?" asked Jack. "His response?"

"In great anger, he talked about blood and position; respect for tradition and place in the community. He believes you belong among the common people and that your skill as a gunman proves that. As he put it, your low background would never permit a union with a daughter of such high position."

"Do you believe any of this, Father?" asked Applejack. "Is this how you see it?"

"Perhaps I did once, when I was very young; but no longer. I believe a man can rise to any position if his energies and knowledge will permit. In short, a poor man can become rich, and a commoner can become a great leader, a poor person, an educated priest and a man of God. As I have. Does that answer your question, my son?"

Applejack was standing, and now he sat down, despondent, head hanging, all the energy seemingly gone from his body.

"It's all way too complicated for me," said Applejack.

"So what?" said the priest. "Life is always complicated."

"I can tell you this," said Jack. "I don't think it will be a betrayal to Maria. I thought she and I had come to an understanding out there on the trail, on the return to her father's hacienda. It was unfortunate he came to us, rather than the two of us going to him. Perhaps it would be best if I just leave. I have been reading about Oregon; maybe I should..."

"Running away will solve nothing."

"Not running, Father; just accepting reality and going some other place to start anew."

"Would you give up so easily?" asked the priest.

"Not easily...but...it seems hopeless."

"Applejack," responded the clergyman. "Now that Marshal Masterson is on your side and working with me, I am confident that we will find a way to help you and your cause with Maria. Just give us some time."

Chapter 19

On the following Saturday night there was a shootout on the streets of Trinidad. Deputy Applejack was involved in a fight with a large group of cowboys and Spanish workers. Flint, Jack's partner, was wounded, as were several of the drunken cowhands. Jack was reluctant to use his pistol. He merely shot into the air and then used it as a club. He came through it without a scratch, and the young gunman's reputation spread further.

One morning, after his round of duty, Applejack went back to his shack to sleep. Bat Masterson's horse was standing at a hitching post in front of the cabin. Opening the door, the deputy's eyes adjusted to the gloom and he saw the marshal sitting at a little table, a lamp lit. In his hand he held a half-empty whiskey bottle.

"Come in, Jack, come on in. And to think that I recommended this dump for you. Well, at least it's cheap and keeps out the rain and cold."

"Father Munnecom said you wanted to speak with me?"

"That's right, kid. I have a whole heap of things I've been storing up to say to you. I know I'm a bit in my cups, but for what I have to say, I needed a drink or two. It sort of oils up my better side, if you know what I mean. Or, perhaps you don't. Shall I pour you a drink?"

"No, sir, unless you happen to have a sarsaparilla."

"As a matter of fact, I do," said Masterson, pulling up a basket from the floor and setting it on the table. "And for good measure, I had a breakfast put together. It's in this basket. Eggs and all the trimmings, including plates and utensils. Here, you set it out, and while you're at it, I'll do the talking."

Hesitantly, Jack took off his hat and hung it on a peg. Pouring water from a pitcher into a basin, Applejack washed his hands and dried them on a towel. Then he walked to the table, opened the lids of the wicker basket, and began setting out plates and utensils for two. Wrapped in cloth on separate plates were the eggs, bacon, and bread. The aroma of the food permeated the cabin. Finished, Jack sat down slowly on the opposite chair and stared across the table at the lawman.

"I bet you're wondering what this is all about. Before I tell you, there are a few things I been hankering to get off my mind."

"Yes?"

"All my life, Applejack, I've stayed away from getting personally involved with other people. I mean, to the extent I could. I've been fortunate coming out West. I started out with my two brothers, Ed and Jim, skinning buffalo hides. It was a messy and gory thing that at least gave me spending money and knowledge of the country. Then I got in that Indian fight at Adobe Walls, and before I knew it, I found I was good with a pistol and rifle, and gained this reputation as a gunfighter. I became a civilian scout for the Army, and eventually ended up a lawman. Along the way, I met a lot of famous Westerners. You've heard of em: the Earps, Doc Holliday, Buffalo Bill, railroad executives—a whole slew of people, including politicians. It helps to know the right people to get ahead in life. But let me tell you this: if a man isn't up to his job, no amount of friends will help a fellow keep his work."

"Impressive, boss, but what does that have to do with me?"

"Be patient, Jack, I'm gettin to it. Let me do it in my own way. You know, when my brother Ed was killed, I was thinking of giving it all up and heading back east. I'm educated enough; I like sports, especially boxing, and I could be a news reporter, and…I bet…a good one."

"Yes, sir?"

"You know what? I like to keep track of people who have the power to change my future. There's a young man named Teddy Roosevelt, the youngest member of the New York State Assembly. A friend writes and tells me to watch out for him and that he's a fellow that's going somewhere, maybe vice president or something like that. That friend has spoken to Roosevelt and urges him to visit the west for himself. Maybe I can figure a way to meet him if he does. No one gets ahead in this world without connections.

"If you say so."

"I do, Jack! What I'm sharing with you is important."

"I'm listening, sir."

"I still think someday I'll go back east. If I don't make it as a reporter, I have it in mind to seek an appointment for US Marshal. It takes knowing someone in power to get a job like that and don't you forget it. Mark you, there isn't another man besides you that I would tell these things to. You know why, Applejack?"

"No sir, I don't."

Marshal Masterson tipped the large whiskey bottle to his lips and took a long drink. Jack could hear the liquid slosh, and the loud swallows. The marshal set the bottle down hard onto the table and some of its liquid splattered up and out across dinner plates and floor. The smell of alcohol filled the air of the small cabin.

"I'll tell you why!" said Masterson, raising his voice. "Because, Jack, I never met no man like you in my entire life. No, let me qualify that: no young man like you. When you saved my life in the Imperial Saloon, I thought it was a fluke. I saw you were down and out and didn't have a penny to your name. I felt sorry for you and thought there might be a slight chance you could use that pistol of yours. And besides…I needed a deputy. Mind you, I wasn't expecting much; but the least you had to do was be able to shoot."

Masterson stopped talking. He lifted the bottle from the table and took another drink. Then he breathed in loudly and let out a long slow alcohol-filled breath. There was complete silence in the room except for the sound of a rising wind outside, whistling in and around the wooden building.

"Yes?" said Applejack, finally breaking the silence.

"Let me tell you, Jack, that I never in my life saw a man shoot as well as you. That goes for my other deputies. And they are a hard fightin lot; but nothin like you. Jack, I never saw a more natural lawman. Mostly you get along with others by keeping your mouth shut. That's a gift; it makes other men wonder."

"I didn't tell you," replied Jack, "but I'm giving up the law."

"You think I don't know that! And it's all over that Spanish gal you've got your heart set on."

"It's not just because of her, sir…"

"I know. You hate what you done. Especially the killing of Bill Peacock."

"Yes, that's the biggest part..."

"And you want to go back to ranching and raising stock so you can afford to take care of that little filly you're so fond of."

"If you know all this," said Jack, "why are you..."

"Now, hold on. I told you, I need to explain this in my own way. Never before have I wanted to help another person like you. I mean...other than my brothers, but they're blood. And backing the Earps and Doc Holliday, well...and the other things in my life...that just fell into my hands. You know it was me that saved Holliday from extradition back to...oh, never mind. But this here, what I'm going to do for you, comes from something else."

"Sir, I didn't ask for help from anyone. I got my own way..."

"Shut up, son, and let me finish! Now, where was I? Oh yes, when I saw you shoot, I saw that in one way, you were better suited to be a lawman than even I. Not the Earps, or Holliday, Hickok, or any gunman in the West is as fast with a revolver as you. I believe that. But what I wondered was, what would happen when you faced a man shooting back. Now, that's the true test. You proved that soon enough..."

"I didn't want to kill him," explained Applejack.

"I know that, kid." Again Masterson took a large swig from the bottle and set it on the table. "Now this is what I have to say. Here you were this boy-man, wet behind the ears, no experience to speak of, straight off the farm. I expected you to act just as we did at your age. When exposed to it, you'd take to drink and loose women just like us. But what did you do? You stuck to milk and sarsaparilla. Instead of joining us at night, you went to your bed. And to top it off, you saved your money and put it in a bank. And on Sundays you attended church, saw that gal, and made friends with a Catholic Priest."

"But sir, it was the way I was raised, and…"

"Let me finish, let me finish! If I don't get it said, I'll never be able to say it again. You surprised me, Applejack. At first I thought you were a wide-eyed, pompous little…but then I saw it was the real thing. Now Wyatt, the Doc, and I are good lawmen, but I'm afraid drink, the ladies, and gambling sullied our reputations a bit. At least with the voters and those that have a say so in such things. Let me tell you, Jack, no other man has given me such fits and…"

"I'll quit now, Mr. Masterson," said Jack. "I've got the money you gave me, and I can start a little spread."

"The Martinez family wouldn't let Maria come anywhere near a hard-scrabble rancher. No, Jack, me and Father Munnecom won't let you do it."

"I don't understand," replied Jack.

"You will. The priest and I had a long talk and he convinced me to help you. Or, I convinced him to… it doesn't matter. Here is what we put together. In a card game, I won a little spread over La Veta way. It's on the Cuchara River. It runs right through the middle of the property and gives you year-round water. You can irrigate and get two cuttings of hay every year. There's a train no further than two miles from the ranch to ship nice fat cattle. And, I hear you can even do a little trout fishing. Anyway, I'm giving you the place, for a price. I have a Mexican caretaker, and he's raising a few head of cattle, some hosses, and his family. I recommend you keep him."

"But all I have is nine hundred dollars and..."

"I'm not asking for any money now; but every year, in December, you send me cash. What you can afford, but no less than one hundred dollars, until I tell you the place is paid for."

"I don't know what to say."

"Say yes."

"Can we go look at the ranch?"

"First thing tomorrow we'll take the train to La Veta and you can meet Saul Hernandez and his family. That alone is worth the trip. Meet me at my office at nine."

The door slammed and Applejack heard the creak of leather and hooves pounding away into the distance. The food lay cold and untouched upon the table. Thoroughly bewildered by what he'd heard and the passage of events, Jack walked over and collapsed on his bed.

Chapter 20

Applejack didn't sleep well, and woke up early. He went about getting washed and dressed. In the back shed, he fed and watered Bucky and his mother's horse. It was January, and the mornings were quite cool. Working in the frosty coldness, he had his mount saddled and ready. When daybreak hit, he rode to the Alpine Restaurant. There he found Masterson and some of the deputies at a table. Jack waved and sat at a counter, ordered breakfast, and ate. Finished, he walked his horse to the marshal's office. With the rising of the sun, the temperature began to warm.

Bat Masterson appeared with his horse, and the two rode to the train station. An attendant was waiting and led them to an open cattle car with a ramp. They watched as the horses were led up the planks. Then trainmen removed the ramp and closed the door. A conductor greeted the well-known marshal with solicitous behavior and even removed his cap. He led them to a passenger car and gave comment.

"Marshal Masterson, any time the Atchison, Topeka and Santa Fe Railway can be of assistance, just call on us. I'll have my men transfer the horses to the D&RG at Walsenburg."

The way Masterson was being treated was impressive, and it gave yet another measure of respect for his boss. Applejack, for the first time in his life, sat in a plush seat and watched and listened as the steam locomotive spewed black smoke. The train chugged slowly into movement, gained momentum, and clattered along at breath-taking speed.

"How fast do you think we are going?" asked Applejack.

Masterson, looked towards his companion and smiled. He stared out the window at the passing landscape and then laughed.

"I bet this is your first train ride. Oh…I reckon we're travelin at about 40 miles an hour."

There was little conversation on the trip to La Veta, and Masterson tipped his hat down and slept while Applejack, not wanting to miss anything, peered out the window at the passing landscape. Coming close to the little town, Jack looked out in wonder. Having seen pictures of Switzerland in a book Father Munnecom had shown him from his large library, the young deputy was impressed with the lavish green mountains and deep valleys. The countryside around La Veta looked similar to those photographs.

The train stopped in the village and the two men got off. Their ride on the Santa Fe Railroad, and West on the Denver & Rio Grande Narrow Gauge was exhilarating to the young man. Removing the horses from the cattle car was somewhat problematic, and the railroad workers in La Veta appeared to give Marshal Masterson trouble. Finally, the task was accomplished.

"Bad blood," growled the marshal. "It's about the Royal Gorge war. Maybe someday I will explain that. But out here, Jack, a fellow takes a side, and win or lose, a man sometimes makes enemies for life. That fight got me a lot of them."

They retrieved their mounts and Masterson began to lead his young deputy toward the ranch he'd won in a poker game. Passing through the sleepy little town, they rode out onto wide open meadows. The surrounding mountains stood above them overlooking the deep valley. They continued northwest for a couple miles and came up to the Cuchara River. Large cottonwoods and other scrub trees grew along the banks. The two men followed a path to an open area of grassland. There were patches of green, despite it being winter, and the temperature was now nearly sixty degrees. Wooden fences surrounded field after field. They saw cattle grazing in one area, and horses in another.

The lawmen stopped and admired the scenery. A hundred yards to their left, on a little hill, stood a wooden cabin and various small buildings. Dogs began barking. Near the house, three men worked at cutting logs into firewood. One of them dropped his saw, walked to a fence, and picked up a rifle. Other rifles quickly appeared. The first ranch hand agilely climbed the fence, jumped down, and walked forward. Masterson spurred his horse and Applejack followed.

As the lawmen approached, the fellow raised his weapon and then recognized Masterson. The man smiled and ran up to meet him.

"Señor Masterson," he said. "So glad to see you."

"Saul Hernandez, meet my deputy, Applejack Martin."

Saul, holding the rifle, came closer and shook the young lawman's hand.

"So good to meet you, Señor Applejack!"

"Same here."

"Come, señores," said Saul. "Come to the house and

114

my wife Rosita will find something for you to eat and drink. It is my great pleasure to see you again, Señor Masterson. My wife and my children will be pleased. You will see."

Word of visitors reached Rosita, and the family came running from the fields and the cabin. In front of the house gathered at least ten children. The oldest were two young men around eighteen, and they appeared to be twins. The other eight seem to range from sixteen to about five years old.

"Say hello to Señores Masterson and Applejack," said the father.

The family shouted out greetings, and a very slim woman with black hair came forward.

"Señores," said Rosita smiling. "Please come in the house and sit at my table, I have pollo y frijoles and good coffee. Children, go back to your chores. The men of the house have important business."

Applejack and Masterson climbed down off their horses and one of the twins took their mounts and led them to hitching posts. The other children complained to their mother and then scattered. A group of chickens came pecking at the ground and passed Jack as he followed his boss into the house. In a matter of a few minutes, coffee in large mugs and plates of warm food were set before the two guests.

"Eat, señores," commanded Rosita. "There is plenty of food. You will like it. Eat and then you and my husband can talk."

Hernandez, smiling, brought his own cup of coffee to the large table and sat across from Bat Masterson. He motioned the two men to partake and then whispered:

"Señores, eat what you can. My Rosita will be upset if you don't like her food. She is a very good cook, but sometimes she can be…difficult."

After the morning's trip, both Jack and the older man were hungry, and they finished the food and the coffee in short order. Rosita hovered near a large stove and looked on.

"Didn't I tell you?" said Rosita. "Would you like more, señores?"

"It was a wonderful lunch, Rosita, but I don't think either one of us can eat any more. Perhaps more coffee?" said Masterson. "And then could you leave us to talk?"

She came with a large coffee pot and filled the three cups.

"I will go, but you send a woman from her kitchen, and that is hard…"

"Rosita!" exclaimed Saul.

His wife raised her hand in an abrupt gesture to her man and then, frowning, she went out through the front door.

"Is this visit something I should be concerned about?" asked Saul in a grave tone of voice.

"Not at all," replied Masterson. "Why don't you talk to Applejack…I am selling the place to him, and if he agrees, he will be your new boss."

"Sir, my family and I would like to work for you, as we have for Marshal Masterson."

"Fine with me," replied Jack. "I see you've put a lot of hard work in the place. It looks good. It seems there's plenty of water and grass. How many acres and how much stock?"

"You know about ranching, Señor Jack?" asked Saul.

"I was raised on a little spread," replied the younger man. "But it was nothing like this. It was mostly rock, little grass, and hardly any water. The stock went hungry and thirsty and it…it was hard."

"Sí, señor, I understand. Here we can raise twice, maybe three times, the cattle as such a place you describe. The ranch is two homesteads, 320 acres, and we have thirty-three cattle and ten horses. But I have written you a message, Señor Masterson. Perhaps that is another reason you are here? We had five cattle stolen by rustlers in the middle of the night. If it wasn't for one of my grown sons, it would have been more. Now we take turns guarding the stock."

"Back east, five grown steers would fetch nearly a hundred fifty dollars," complained Masterson. "That's quite a loss."

"Sí," said Saul. "If Señor Jack comes and stays, an extra hand who can shoot would be a very good thing. I am afraid it may get worse. The bigger ranches have suffered. Cattle thieves have stolen much, always in the middle of the night."

"Saul, if you lose more cattle, send me a wire," said Masterson. "I want to know. Now tell me, where can Jack live?"

"We have a little cabin west of here," replied Saul. "We can fix it up and…"

"I can't give up my deputy right now, but by April, I don't expect to be in office any more. That's in about four months. If he buys the ranch, he can take over then."

Both Applejack and Hernandez nodded their heads yes.

"We have to meet the return train," said the marshal.

"You guard the place well. And let me tell you, amigo, you will be getting a new boss who is a real pistolero."

"If Señor Masterson says this is so, I believe it," said Saul. "As I said, we need such a man on this ranch."

The Hernandez family came quickly when they saw the three men step out onto the porch. The two visitors took to their horses. Everyone shouted their goodbyes and Applejack and the marshal rode back along the river, southeast towards La Veta.

"What do you think, Jack?" asked Masterson.

"I've never seen such a spread, and with so much water. Even in winter some of the grass stays green."

"It is something, isn't it?" said the older lawman. "And the mountains shelter and protect it. When it does rain, the water runs down onto the lowland. But it still lacks what you need to impress Martinez."

"More land," said Applejack. "Enough to raise a large herd for market."

"Yes, a spread sufficient to impress that arrogant father. Here land costs are double, triple, what they are in other places. I think if Martinez saw it, even he would be impressed."

"It really is a splendid place."

Bat Masterson laughed.

"If you need help acquiring more land, perhaps Father Munnecom can think of something."

The cool morning wind had stopped and both men enjoyed their ride back to the train.

Chapter 21

One Sunday morning after policing the town, instead of going to sleep, Applejack, full of restless energy, saddled Bucky and rode out onto the dry prairie. Following cattle and deer trails, he wandered south and found himself on a hill overlooking the Martinez's hacienda. It was a large place, and looking down into the walled garden, he saw it was well watered from a pond not too far from the estate. Jack dismounted and held reins and sat on a wide rock. Tying the reins to a bush, the young deputy laid down on the flat stone. In the growing warmth of the day, he fell asleep.

The attack was vicious and without warning. His only crimes were Applejack's affection for the young woman and his unwanted presence. Jack was struck with the hard handle of a quirt, another horsewhip belonging to the merciless father.

"So," shouted Martinez. "The boy has come to spy. I knew I would be speaking with you soon!"

"No need to hit me while I was resting," replied Applejack, wiping blood from a cut on his forehead.

"I will strike any interloper that comes between me and my daughter! You are not wanted here. I wonder if I should let you live. Even your law says it is permissible to shoot trespassers."

Behind Señor Martinez were the two vaqueros who guarded the rich rancher, Carlos and Juan. Both men were tall and well armed. They stood some distance away, hands on pistol butts.

Applejack drew and fanned his revolver. The sombrero of the closest vaquero, named Carlos, flew off his head. Holding his .45, Jack backed up. Untying reins, he quickly mounted. Looking down, he covered the three men.

"I will not fight Maria's father," responded the young deputy, "but I could easily defeat the three of you."

"Once again you dare to use my daughter's given name," bellowed the enraged Martinez. "To you it will always be Señorita Martinez!"

"Too much has passed between us for Maria to forget me, or for me to forget her. Someday she and I will be married."

"And what will you offer her, gringo?" questioned the angry father. "A pig's wallow? A dirty little ranch with a filthy cabin, and a bunch of sickly cattle? No, señor, you're not worthy to touch the hem of her skirt. You will always remain on your knees, a common person, born to low parents and poor circumstances. Go! Never ride onto my land again, or next time you shall not be so lucky."

"I am the one holding the pistol, Mister Martinez, and it is you who are lucky."

With that, Applejack fanned two more shots which struck the holsters and pistols of the guards. Both revolvers went flying away from torn leather. Then the young gunman turned his horse, applied heels to its flanks, and galloped away, .45 still in hand.

"Señor Martinez," said one of the vaqueros, stooping and picking up his revolver and torn holster. "Shall we chase him down?"

"From a distance, and with a rifle, perhaps you could

shoot him," said the rich rancher. "But face-to-face, I am afraid there is not a man in all of Colorado that could. No, let him go. You have to respect a fellow who bests three armed men. Even if he is a filthy gringo."

Angry, Applejack raced Bucky across dry grassland, avoiding great clumps of prickly pear and jumping cholla. When he reached his shack, he hopped down. Still furious, he knew enough to care for his beloved horse. Stopping to remove saddle and blanket, he walked Bucky and, when he was cooled, he took a rag and wiped the horse down and led him into the barn with the mare.

If drink and getting drunk were something he did, he would certainly have participated on this day. Still, without sufficient sleep, he entered his little cabin. He washed up and changed clothes, getting ready for his four o'clock meeting with Father Munnecom. And, for the first time since the sessions had begun, the deputy had not read the assigned book.

The priest met Applejack at the front door of his private quarters.

"You have been fighting!" exclaimed the priest.

"I wouldn't call it that," replied Jack.

"Explain."

The young man told his older friend what had occurred.

"You take chances," said the priest, frowning. "I think you may have made matters worse."

"At least I know how it is with her father."

"Jimena!" shouted the priest, and the housekeeper came running.

The Father told her to bring antiseptic and a clean cloth. While he looked on, the housekeeper dabbed and cleaned the swollen wound on Applejack's forehead.

"Why do you take such action when I told you to wait and allow Masterson and me to handle this matter?"

"I was restless," responded Jack, "and besides, I thought it would be harmless."

"Don't you know that Martinez guards his ranch with the fierceness of a mountain lion? Among the Mexican people, it is well known that he gives no quarter. He does not lose cattle to rustlers, and they know to stay away, or be hanged on the spot."

"I thought he only talked tough," replied Applejack.

"No, he's a ruthless man of action. I am afraid it will take a great deal to calm him down."

"He made it clear he doesn't like me."

"From what you describe, you found a clever way to escape. You are lucky you did, because I am certain you would have been whipped, or worse. But then, I know Martinez. He respects strength and courage; and you showed both. No…perhaps…there was something gained. You bested him when so few could."

"Whatever, Father."

"Did Masterson show you the ranch?"

"You know about that? Yes, and it sure has plenty of water. But it's short on acreage."

"Before you retire from your job as deputy marshal, perhaps there is a way I can help you."

"How?"

"Patience, my son, patience," replied the priest.

The rest of the afternoon the two discussed various subjects other than the one most pressing on the young man's mind. When Applejack left to get ready for his night patrol, he was in a better frame of mind. The priest had that effect upon him.

It wasn't more than an hour into their patrol when Flint and Applejack saw a horse gallop through town and skid to a halt before them. It was a woman dressed as a man, in Spanish garb and wearing a pistol at her waist.

"Applejack!" cried the woman.

Jack recognized Maria's voice, and he was very surprised. The vaquero outfit she was wearing did nothing to hide her woman's figure. In fact, it enhanced it. Applejack and Flint both stared, eyes wide, mouths open. Jack couldn't recall ever seeing Maria looking prettier. She removed her sombrero and a tumble of black shining hair cascaded down her back. Under the streetlamps her face was lit with a soft beauty that would take any man's breath away.

"Please help me! Rustlers, they have attacked our herd, and when Father and his men tried to stop them, he was captured."

"How many?" asked Applejack.

"I don't know."

Maria was not riding sidesaddle, and she raised one leg over the Spanish pommel and jumped to the ground. Holding reins, she stepped forward and up to Applejack.

"I know what happened today, and I know my father treated you terribly. And…you were lucky to get away. But please, for my sake, help me save him."

"Maria," asked Applejack, "do you know which way they went?"

"All I know is that our men were shot up and few escaped. Pedro, badly wounded, came to the casa and said there were many cattle thieves, and that they captured my papa and took him with them."

"We're town marshals, ma'am," said Flint. "We have no jurisdiction..."

"Go for Masterson," said Applejack. "He'll tell us what we can do. Besides, we need him and all the deputies..."

"I think you're asking too much," replied Flint.

"They're criminals, aren't they?" said Jack. "You can do what you want, but I'm going with her."

"What can one gun do?" asked Flint. "Jack, you hold off long enough for me to get the marshal. He's up at the Imperial. I'll see what he says."

In Flint's absence, Maria stood before Applejack and said nothing. Stepping down off the walk, the deputy took her horse's reins and tied them to the hitch rail. Turning, he held her hand, and then she rushed forward and put her arms around him. Surprised, he embraced her.

"Oh, Jack, it is all so terrible. What my father has done and said to you, and now he is..."

"Maria, I don't think the marshal will fail us. But we need men, and there is no other person who can raise a posse faster than him."

"After today—I mean, what father did—have you given up on me?"

"Didn't he tell you? I said that too much has passed between us, and that I am going to marry you."

"You said that? To my father? Ohh, Jack. Hold me tight..."

Jack squeezed her, bent down, and kissed her. They were caught in an embrace when Masterson and Flint came running.

"Flint has told me, señorita," said Masterson. "What

do you think we can do?"

"Señor Marshal," said Maria. "Please, whatever men you can find, I will lead them back to our ranch, and Pedro can tell you what he knows."

"Will you pay for men?" asked the marshal. "It would make it easier."

"Sí," replied the young woman. "I will."

"Do you want the cattle recovered?" asked Masterson.

"I am sure Father cares, but I don't. Please, I will pay anything within reason for help."

"Flint," ordered Masterson. "Go to the bar. In the back room is my brother James and two deputies. Jim's visiting. Tell him I'd take it kindly if he and the deputies would police the town until we get back. On the way, look for men for a posse. Jack and I will try to recruit as many fellows as we can. You have fifteen minutes; go!"

Flint hurried away and Bat Masterson crossed to the center of the street, drew his pistol, and fired it three times. Lamps began to be lit at various businesses and merchants came from back rooms to see what was transpiring. Men came from bars, and as they looked on, the marshal fired another shot and then began reloading his weapon. Curious, a crowd formed.

"I appreciate your response," shouted Masterson. "Not too far from here, a cattle herd has been rustled and a man taken. The sheriff is out of town. In his stead, I'm calling for men to form a posse! We're paying ten dollars a man. If you're coming, grab warm gear, ammunition, your weapons, and a horse! We'll meet up here in fifteen minutes."

The crowd murmured responses and quickly dispersed.

"Jack," said Masterson. "Go get your horse and bring a

rifle and fill your saddlebags with ammunition. Bring warm clothing and that extra pistol I gave you. Maria will be safe here. In a moment, I'll have to get my gear."

"Señor Marshal," said Maria, "I am very grateful."

"Let's see how big a posse we can get, before you thank me," replied Masterson. "We'll be lucky to find cattle tracks in the dark."

"Pedro will know where the cattle and father were ambushed."

"We'll need a tracker," replied the lawman. "Give me a moment, I'll go back to the Imperial and send someone for the man I have in mind. Wait for me."

Maria replaced her sombrero, tucking her long hair underneath it. Sitting on the steps of the walk, she watched and listened as men scurried back and forth across the street. Applejack was the first to return with his horse and full saddlebags. A rifle and scabbard was attached to his saddle, and he now wore two pistols.

"Where's the marshal?" asked Jack.

"He said he would find someone to track, and he needed his horse and…"

"Good."

"Everything is happening so fast," said Maria. "Jack, do you think…"

"I am sure the marshal will do everything possible to get your father back."

Men leading horses began to gather. Many wore pistols and carried rifles in scabbards. Others, including several merchants, held rifles in hand. Some of these weapons were from the Great Conflict. Jack recognized a Springfield, a Sharps, a Henry, and even a seven-shot Spencer.

Not more than fifteen minutes later, Masterson appeared in a warm jacket, leading his horse. Mounting, he sat and counted by pointing his finger at each man.

"Eighteen will have to do. Men, I promise you nothing but a hard ride, possible action, and ten dollars. You're under my command now, and you will do exactly what I say, or face me. I caution you, there will be no quitters. If you want to drop out, do it now."

One of the older men, who was holding a Springfield rifle, laughed.

"I might not be as spry as I once was, young feller, but I still can shoot this old musket. Let's get her done."

Maria untied her horse and waited next to the marshal and Applejack.

"Men," shouted Masterson. "This is Señorita Martinez; she will be leading us to her ranch."

Maria mounted her horse, and each member of the posse mounted theirs. She spurred her animal, and it jumped to a trot and then very quickly into a gallop. Horses fell in line as they rushed through town and west onto the open prairie. Within a half hour, they crossed the grounds of the ranch and eventually arrived at the walled hacienda.

Coming to a wide gate, they found it open. Inside the courtyard were paved stones. Upon the paving lay wounded and dead vaqueros. Attending to the injured men were several housemaids, along with a dozen or more ranch hands. The posse dismounted and stood along the outside wall while Maria, Masterson, Applejack, and Flint entered the courtyard.

Maria searched and found Pedro, who lay on blankets next to the entrance of the large house. She knelt, and

Masterson and his deputies stood over them.

"Pedro, I am so sorry you are injured. If you can, please tell me, do you know where they have taken Father?" she asked in Spanish.

Pedro opened his eyes and responded. "Señorita, the rustlers swept him along with the cattle. If you hurry, you will catch them. The herd was taken near the big pond. You know where that is. They headed west."

Applejack looked around, and through the gate he saw an Indian approach. He touched Masterson's sleeve.

"Blackhorse Charley!" said the marshal. "Thanks for coming so quickly. It's this girl's father and a herd of cattle we're after."

"I will find," said the Indian.

"Charley's a Ute, and one of the best trackers I know," explained Masterson. "He'll locate your father, Maria. If any man can, it will be him."

Coffee and fresh water was offered to the posse. In short order, Maria explained their intent to her vaqueros.

"You've done all you can, Miss," said Masterson. "Suppose you stay here and take care of your wounded men."

"I can ride and shoot as well as any man," said Maria Martinez, putting on a warm coat. "And no matter what you say, I go too!"

Bat Masterson looked to Applejack, who raised no objection.

"I was afraid of that," complained the lawman. "Jack, if you can't stop her, I guess I won't, either."

"It is her father," said Applejack. "Any one of us would demand the same thing. Besides, I bet she can shoot as well as she rides."

The town marshal shrugged his shoulders and walked out of the courtyard. He signaled for the posse to grab their horses. By the time the men mounted, temperatures had dropped and a cold wind was blowing and increasing in strength. With the addition of the Martinez vaqueros, the posse of eighteen had now grown to thirty-one. Maria told Blackhorse Charley the location of the pond and where the cattle were rustled.

The Indian tracker led the way. Riding across open prairie in the dark was always a risky thing. Dropoffs, cliffs, and holes in the ground could cause horse and man to fall to their death. For many hours the men followed single file, cautious how and where they rode. They climbed over a mountain pass and into an open valley. There they found a cattle trail. Once on it, the big Ute pushed his horse harder and the armed party moved faster over level ground.

Blackhorse Charley led the armed men west, finding tracks and sign in the dark that no other man could see. They reached trampled grass and discovered which direction the large rustled herd had gone. Following at a quick pace, the hours passed, and then they came to rocky ground. The blowing wind increased, and stars and moon could no longer be seen, as the night sky was covered in clouds. It became pitch dark and the Indian halted the posse. Charley dismounted, twisted some grass, and lit it. Using the light, he looked closely at the ground and determined which direction to take.

The thirty-one men followed slowly behind the tracker and the hours passed. They came to a wall of rock and halted their forward movement. The lone Indian continued studying the scarred rocks. In the east, predawn lit the sky enough for the Ute to see. Clouds swirled above, and the wind increased to speeds that made it difficult to stand or sit astride a horse. Then it began to spit blowing snow, and soon it became a whiteout.

Applejack, riding near Maria, gathered his slicker and put it over her. He had gloves and he gave them to her to put on. The wind was so fierce, it required them to take their bandannas and tie them over their head gear. Many a hat was lost, including Maria's magnificent sombrero. She tied a scarf under her chin to cover her ears.

"We are near the herd," Blackhorse Charley shouted into Masterson's ear. "Best to leave men with the horses, tie them good, and go through this pass on foot. The weather hides our presence. But no one can see to fight."

Bat Masterson passed the message, until each man understood. Then the marshal asked for rope and instructed the men to cut hobbles and tie them to the front legs of every mount. He selected two of the older men to tie reins together and guard the horses. There was some argument from the man with the Springfield. Masterson said something that caused the fellow to submit to the task. The remaining posse followed Blackhorse Charlie through the narrow opening in the rock and down a sloping trail. To keep together, each person in the party had to hold on to the one in front. The snowstorm made it nearly impossible to see more than a few feet in any direction.

Entering a deep valley, a cacophony of sound filled the ears of the posse. The wind and swirling snow roared, cattle bellowed, and somewhere ahead, a horse screamed.

"We are here," said Blackhorse Charley to Masterson,

"but no one can see."

"Find us shelter, and we'll hunker down and wait," ordered the marshal.

Blackhorse Charley led the way. The posse moved slowly in the direction the Indian tracker led them. Coming to a long ridge of rock, each person easily heard the bellowing and complaining cattle, which seemed to be very near. Collapsing to the ground, the posse followed the Indian's example. Each person dug away drifting snow, and sat down. The ridge of stone protected them from the hard blowing northerner, but did little to keep the falling snow off their bodies. It was becoming brutally cold, and those without sufficient clothing suffered.

"We can't keep sitting here without building a fire," said Applejack to the Indian and Masterson.

"Can't build fire if a man can't find wood," said Charley, stating the obvious.

"Huddle together, or freeze!" said the marshal.

The word was spread. The freezing posse huddled back to back to keep as warm as possible. Some of the men were clever enough to have taken their horse blankets from under their saddles. The group shivered and tried its best to endure the cold as the sky slowly began to lighten. From time to time, the wind lessoned; and in those moments it was possible to see further distances.

The snow finally slowed and stopped. The wind continued to blow, but not as hard as before. The posse looked over the wall of rock. They could see cattle lying or standing, their backs to the wind. Across the valley, smoke was rising from a cabin. Now they knew where the rustlers were located and where Martinez may be held.

Shivering, Masterson looked to Blackhorse Charley. Blowing on his hands to warm them, he whispered: "We have to look out for guards, if there are any. What do you think?"

"No guards in this storm," said Charley.

"How will we get my father out of the cabin alive?" asked Maria.

"We will do our best," replied Masterson. "That's all we can do."

"When we get there," said Applejack, "I'll enter the shack first and try to get him out."

"Just what I expected," said the marshal. "We'll think of something, Jack. You know there are a lot of guns here, and you don't have to do this by yourself."

"Got that right," said Flint.

Glad to be on the move, at a signal from Masterson, the men arose. Following the tracker, the marshal, Applejack, Maria, and Flint led the posse forward. They bent over and in single file crossed the snow covered plain to the cattle herd. Then, at the marshal's signal, the men went past the herd, separated, and formed a circle around the cabin.

The log building had been added to, and was larger than it looked. Walking around it, Masterson saw another door built onto the rear addition. He signaled men to cover the back. Returning to the front of the cabin, he directed Maria to stay with Blackhorse Charley. Applejack, Flint, and Masterson moved toward the log building. Jack put hand to the latch and opened the door. A wall of warmth struck his body, and then he entered.

The windows were shuttered against the cold, and the interior was dark.

"Close that door!" shouted one of the outlaws. "It's cold! You trying to freeze us out?"

Applejack, seeing little, ran through the interior to the back door and kicked it open. More light poured into the cabin, and with that, the rustlers stirred to action. They jumped from their beds. Pistols were grabbed, and Jack fanned his revolver and shot down two outlaws. Flint and Masterson stood inside near the door, covering the young deputy's every move. Two rustlers, shooting wildly, rushed from their bunks towards the front door. Flint killed one and Masterson the other. Four other armed outlaws ran out the back and were instantly shot down by a fusillade of bullets.

Applejack holstered his empty pistol and grabbed his spare. Standing in the gloom of the cabin was an outlaw holding a revolver to Alfonso Martinez's head.

"Hold it!" yelled the rustler. "One more step and I'll shoot him! Bring two horses and I'll let him go once we're away."

"I'm to believe that?" asked Applejack.

Bat Masterson moved to the right and Flint moved to Jack's left. Both had their pistols in hand.

"Let him go," said the young deputy to the rustler, "and you'll live."

"To be taken outside and hung? No I don't think so. Get the horses. Now!"

"You!" exclaimed Martinez to Applejack. "Of all the peeples, it had to be you!"

"Shut up," exclaimed the rustler, and he tapped his prisoner's head with the barrel of his pistol. Blood trickled down onto the rich cattle owner's face.

At that exact moment, Applejack fanned his pistol twice. One bullet struck the forehead of the outlaw and the other grazed the ear of Alfonso Martinez. The rustler dropped his weapon and fell backwards onto the dirt floor. Señor Martinez drooped his head, his hands still tied behind his back. Jack holstered his revolver, grabbed a knife, and cut the rope on Martinez's wrists. The wounded man rubbed circulation back into each hand. Then he felt and found a bullet notch in his right ear. Blood flowed copiously. Taking his handkerchief, the rancher attempted to stop the bleeding.

"You...you...gringo!" shouted Martinez in a voice of utter contempt. "You shot me!"

"Consider us even," replied Applejack.

Maria rushed into the cabin, pistol in hand, and followed the sound of her father's voice. She ran up to him and gave him a fierce hug.

"Maria!" shouted the father. "You are dressed as a man! And with a pistola! You shame me, you shame the family..."

Marshal Masterson, walked up to Alfonso Martinez and pushed Maria away. Then he punched the Spanish land owner. The ungrateful father stepped backwards. His body struck the wall, preventing him from falling. His hand went to his jaw.

"Shut up, you old fool!" exclaimed Bat Masterson. "Your daughter went to great lengths to save your arrogant hide, and this is the thanks you give her? And Applejack saved your life. I'm beginning to think none of this was worth it. Outside are over thirty men who volunteered to come in a snowstorm to rescue you! Say another word…and so help me…I'll shoot you myself."

Maria stood beside Masterson, and she hung her head and began to cry, her father's harsh reproof still ringing in her ears. Applejack went up to her and put a consoling arm around her waist.

"Flint!" ordered Masterson. "Call the men in here. When you can, add fuel to the fire and see if you can get them warmed up. Maria, Jack; try to find coffee and food. If we have to, we can shoot a steer. No one is leaving here until we are warm and fed."

With an expression of arrogance and stubborn pride, Señor Alfonso Martinez stood leaning against the log cabin wall. Angry, he continued glaring at his daughter, Applejack, and the marshal. As ordered, he said nothing.

The dozen vaqueros stayed behind in the canyon with the cattle. They used the log cabin to warm themselves, rest, and prepare to return to the ranch with the large herd. For the others, it was a long cold ride to the hacienda where Masterson followed Maria and her father into their home. The marshal demanded and was finally paid two hundred dollars. Then the armed group rode back to town. Before they separated, as promised, the marshal paid the posse.

Chapter 22

Through the cold winter months, activities in town lessoned, and so did crime. The cowhands visited Trinidad, but not as frequently. Miners and travelers still passed through, but in lesser numbers. There were only occasional drunken episodes. Lawlessness was greatly curtailed by the vigilance and accurate guns of Marshal Bat Masterson and his deputies.

On April 3, 1883, Bat Masterson was defeated in a vote for re-election. The count was 647 against and 247 in favor of retaining him for marshal of Trinidad. Voted out of office, Masterson had little reason for staying except for his young friend, Applejack Martin. Once again, the famous lawman appeared at Jack's cabin; this time influenced only a little by drink.

"You should have heard that priest defend you," exclaimed Masterson. "Applejack, one way or another, that arrogant Martinez is going to have to let you marry his daughter. After all, you saved them both, and every person we know, Spanish speaking or not, is on your side."

"Are you sure?" asked Jack.

"You didn't let me finish. The priest and I made a call on that fool of a father. At first he was a complete...but you should have heard what that priest told him."

"Yes?" questioned Applejack, not knowing what else to say.

"That pig-headed old man said you were not worthy.

Father Munnecom told him, in no uncertain terms, that if it wasn't for you, he'd have no life and no daughter. Then Martinez said you were not a gentleman, and the good Father explained that you were as smart as a whip, and that you could keep company with any man in the state. That priest out talked Martinez! Said you were as devout and decent as any man he ever met. Someday, he said, given the chance, you would become a very great..."

"I'm afraid he exaggerated..."

"Let me finish, Jack," replied Masterson. "The gist of it is this: From the beginning, it was Father Munnecom who convinced me that no matter where I am, I can use a yearly income from you rather than selling the little ranch outright. And the Priest persuaded Señor Martinez to at least travel to the ranch and take a look. We did that yesterday, on the train."

"You did?" exclaimed Jack. "What happened?"

"Martinez saw the place, and even that Spanish buzzard was impressed. We toured the ranch, went to town, and Martinez has already made arrangements to buy more land. And, as I speak, he's sending for construction materials to build you and Maria a house. The way he said it: 'My daughter must live to the style she has become accustomed,' or some such rot."

Jack abruptly stood up and began to pace back and forth in the narrow confines of the room. Masterson pulled a flask from a jacket pocket and took a swig. Then the older man began to laugh out loud. Jack stopped and stared at his former boss.

"Well, boy!" shouted Masterson. "You should be whooping it up by now. 'Cause it looks like you're gettin that Martinez gal. And on top of that, the ranch and house of your dreams! If I were you, I'd take some of that money of yours, go to the tailor, and have some suits made. 'Cause son...you sure are going to need them. Stiff collar and all!"

The former marshal laughed again, then abruptly headed for the door. He opened it and stopped to look back at Applejack.

"Kid!" said Masterson. "Now you have no excuse for not sending me money for the ranch each year. I'll wire you cables in December telling you where I'm at."

"I'll do as you say," replied Applejack.

"You better!" replied Masterson. "Son, I don't know if you're the luckiest feller I ever met, or not. But be careful what you wish for. Because, before the month's out, I bet you're going to be cinched, hamstringed, and in debt to one of the meanest and hardest father-in-laws I ever met! Haw, haw!"

The door slammed and then Applejack heard leather squeak and hooves pounding away into the distance. Then the hoofbeats returned and a stentorian voice shouted.

"Boy! You better learn Spanish, or you'll never fit in! And if you think I'm going to the wedding, you got another thought coming! Have a good life, my friend!"

Steel rang on stones and hooves pounded away.

Trying to take it all in, Applejack walked to the door and watched the horse and the man, wearing a derby hat and black suit, disappear up the street. When Bat Masterson was gone, the young man paced, full of nervous energy. Eventually he collapsed in a chair. There he sat, looking at the bare wall. The lovely vision of the form and face of Maria came to him. It was of that moment when she was standing before him in her sombrero, belt and pistol over fancy vaquero garb. Applejack smiled. His desire to be with her for the rest of his life was beyond measure. And he thought, *What could ever go wrong, marrying such an exciting woman as her?*

Dear Reader,
If you enjoyed reading *Applejack & Bat Masterson: Trinidad's Law*, please help promote it by composing and posting a review on Amazon.com.

Charlie Steel may be contacted at
cowboytales@juno.com
or by writing to him at the following address:

Charlie Steel
c/o Condor Publishing, Inc.
PO Box 39
Lincoln, Michigan 48742

Warm greetings from Condor Publishing, Inc.
Gail Heath, publisher